CONVERSATIONS IN THE ABYSS

BY
MICHAEL BROOKES

COPYRIGHT

This is a work of fiction, all resemblances to any persons living or dead is totally a coincidence.

© 2013 Michael Brookes – All rights reserved. Yes all of them.

Dedicated to my good friends David Spaul and Umit Ozturk.

Thanks to my test readers and the Eurogamer writing crew, your comments and advice have been invaluable.

A shout out to Kristen Stone for her handy editing skills: http://www.kristen-stone-the-writer.com/

And of course thanks to everyone for reading my stories!

Keep up my latest news on my blog: http://thecultofme.blogspot.co.uk/

And on Twitter: @TheCultofMe

Prologue

In the beginning

Before the beginning nothing existed. No matter, no energy, not even time. This was not emptiness, for emptiness implies the existence of something, even if it is only the absence of something. Not even the possibility of anything existed.

Without prior warning the point appeared. What once was zero now became all what did and would ever exist. The single point possessed no external boundary or limit. All that existed; all that would ever exist, resided within the singularity.

When the absolute null became something, time came into existence. Not time in the peculiar objective fashion imagined by human beings. Instead it was a concept much stranger, far more complex. This form of time did more than provide a linear sequencing of events. The more malleable time allowed the development of forms mere energy and matter alone could never produce.

The greatest wonder of all was that the entity identified itself. From the first moment of its existence it was self. The single point understood that it was a being of thought. It was a self sufficient entity possessing the ability to reason. However the being lacked a wider context. It knew no external reference. All that existed, that would ever exist, did so within the encapsulation of its self.

The being's awareness defined the reality of existence.

The strange multi-faceted time which made human perception look dull and lifeless unfolded as the being examined itself. As it studied itself the entity transformed. No longer a simple point, the internal structure divided and continued dividing. Every thought triggered a new change. From the impossible external view the sentience remained a singular totality. From its own perspective the entity developed. Not in size, but in complexity. At first simple geometries split inside forming an evolving tableau of mathematical perfection.

The being perceived this transformation and was pleased.

This feeling presented a new experience for the entity. The emotion was not caused by a bio-chemical reaction, but by a process more fundamental. The sensation coloured the being's development adding to structural changes with tints and hue.

The being continued its development. It devised ever more complex schemes with which to express its thoughts. The sentience mastered control over the time analogue, allowing the being to marvel at its creations both from where they began and into what they would become. With this facility the sentience observed the changes at any point in between.

After countless explorations the being realised it didn't just observe instances along the continuum, it existed in all instances at once. The being marvelled at this understanding and explored it further.

By now the singularity consisted of multitudes of galleries in different expressions of form. It no longer limited these expressions to static or simple geometries, but instead created evolving systems which changed according to their initial configuration. It experimented with convoluted structures within their own volumes. Each expanded and collapsed dimensions with fractal perfection.

As the being explored the properties of these shapes, it created an analogue of light. This inspired secondary creations utilizing properties such as projection and occlusion. These in turn created shadows and other effects which possessed no existence in themselves yet were clearly observable.

For aeons the being continued to explore, delving deeper and deeper within itself. Although still a point it encountered no limit to how far it was able to travel and sub-divide within itself. Eventually the entity tired of whimsical discovery and embarked upon a process of consolidation. The entity shaped itself with more coherence, simpler versions of which had been engineered in the enthusiasm of its earliest creations.

The being created itself a home, a place of existence where the being now dwelt. Within the environs of this creation it explored. After an epoch it had created the perfect abode, its own form creating a universe of exquisite complexity. It still lacked understanding of the greatest mystery, what was it?

Despite the lack of understanding the sentience discovered contentment.

From the branching ribbon of the time analogue the entity realised such contentment would be short lived. So the entity examined its own existence. It didn't know the human concept of loneliness, but it learned the sensation.

It created new beings, perfect forms derived from the architecture of itself. It gave these new creations an understanding of themselves and the reality they were born into. They were individuals who, combined, represented the totality of its self. One day humans would call these individuals angels. These angels of the first founding would ultimately grow in to the arch-angels of legend. Each being unique and designed to explore one specific aspect of their creator's existence.

For a long time the angels enjoyed a unity with their creator.

Chapter 1

Tormented in grace

The miracle's fire consumed me.
How long had I been imprisoned here?
Weeks?
Months?
Years?

I knew it was 2011 when the Friar and his team chained me to that monastery wall, but what year was it now?

For too long the chill stone had encased my body and spirit. At first the principal torment had been the miracle. I thought stealing it was a good idea at the time. The blessing had sustained Lazarus for over twenty centuries; the thought it might do the same for me had been a beguiling one. Lazarus had been hell bent on starting the apocalypse and destroying mankind so he could be returned to Heaven. Along the way he'd made the mistake of torturing me.

That memory haunted me still. The moment that I learned that there were people in this world with talents greater than mine.

Naturally I'd inflicted my revenge, stealing the curse others labelled a miracle in the process. Unfortunately the theft came with a cost. The price came in the form of the agony blazing through my wasted flesh. This blessing of eternal life didn't appreciate being worn by another's skin. The price started immediately weakening me while the Friar, Hammond and his soldiers imprisoned me in the walls of the monastery.

The feel of the sun upon my skin soon faded into a distant memory. Now the only connection I had to the outside world came in the form of muffled chants of the monks. Their hymns and constant prayers seeped through the walls like damp. Their sacred words combined with the mask fixed to my face and together prevented my spirit from leaving my body.

How I missed having the ability to soar. I yearned to once again roam high above the earth. The world laid out below me as if I flew like a bird. I could do that at will once. I hadn't used that ability enough.

Even more I missed being able to invade the minds of those I encountered. With a thought I experienced their memories as if they were my own. I could also bend their will with my own like puppets on a string.

At first the miracle and confinement were the only torments I was forced to endure. Strange as it may seem I got used to the suffering. They almost became companions. As time passed new pain entered my world. These started as mundane complaints, hunger pangs in my belly, dryness and then constriction in my throat from thirst. These mundane torments provided some diversion for my bored mind.

For a time I used my gifts to suppress these pains. Eventually the desires of the body overcame my will and along with the miracle they danced through me. They complimented each other, kept my body wracked and my mind desolate.

Even for me depression and despair proved difficult to hold at bay. My state of mind became a serious concern. The pain simply wouldn't end. My mind began to crumble under the relentless assault.

I needed something to distract me. Anything that I could focus my mind on, to separate myself from the twisted pains defining my reality. I sought a refuge and turned to the place that almost spelled my doom many years ago.

The abyss became my escape. On the shadowed cliffs above the veil below I found a new home. I didn't escape the pain completely, but I could hide from it for a while. Sooner or later the pain always dragged me back to my tormented flesh. But for periods of time I freed myself. I delved so deep within myself I reached the very edge of life.

The abyss itself remained a mystery to me. I now realised it wasn't the portal to Hell I'd once assumed. After defeating Lazarus I'd glimpsed Hell as his soul was dragged into the pit. When I stared down into the abyss it wasn't the same. This was the veil between our lives and what comes next.

More than I had during my earlier life, I considered what that meant. What would come next? I couldn't deny some afterlife existed beyond death. Not that I really had to worry about that particular fate. After all, the miracle protected me.

As well as my sanctuary, the abyss eventually turned out to be another of my tormentors. Beyond the veil I discerned vague forms moving in the shadows.

I'd first discovered the abyss in my younger days after taking acid. As it had back then the forms became agitated by my presence. Beyond those depths was the ultimate escape. An escape denied me by the miracle. It made me immortal. Or pretty damn close to it.

There was no escape in any direction for me.

Chapter 2

Warnings from tainted lips

Friar Francis sipped the strong bitter coffee while he waited for his friend to arrive. He loved Rome, although too much time had passed since his last visit. The ancient city always felt like home and this was the perfect time of year to visit. The spring sun warmed the air as the tourist crowds walked by. Across the square the Friar saw his old friend climb from a taxi.

"Some things don't change."

"Unfortunately we do," the Friar responded.

Friar Francis rose and they shook hands warmly. The waiter arrived before they sat and the Friar ordered two coffees. They both drank their coffees as black as the cassocks they wore.

"Do you remember when we first started drinking here?"

"Yes, learning of demons in classes and escaping here into the light to watch the world go by."

Father Moran smiled. "The view is just as pleasant as it was back then."

"It's been too long Ian. Where have you been for the past two years?"

"The society has kept me busy in Africa. I've been with a team helping the local churches. Interesting work, but it involved more pastoral and care work than my usual line of work."

"Cause for celebration surely?" the Friar commented.

"Of course. Most of the cases were simple self-delusion, or symptoms of mental illness. A few turned out to be deliberate cons, a way to get some free medical care."

"Was it really that bad?"

"In some places. For some villages the church provides the only local medical care. And of course the continuing famine causes more hardship." He sipped his coffee. "Having seen some of the hardships they have to suffer, I can't really blame them."

He accepted a cigarette from the Friar and they both lit up. A young passer-by scowled at them in disgust. They both smirked at the woman in reply.

"In the three years I spent in Africa, I saw only one genuine case."

"And is that why you're back in Rome?"

"Yes, but more pertinently here to see you."

"Me?"

"Yes my old friend. The last case was genuine, but the demon said some things which made me think of you."

That surprised the Friar. "What did the demon say?"

"It's probably best to tell you the whole story." He extinguished his cigarette and drained his coffee. "I was officiating at Sunday Mass in one of the small village churches. More of a hut really, but almost the entire village squeezed themselves in. You can't believe how hot the air got in there.

"Anyway, midway through the mass the door suddenly opened and a young man stumbled in. I didn't recognise him, nor did any of the congregation so I guessed he wasn't a local. The village constable later confirmed my assumption.

"As he entered the church he started to scream and collapsed gibbering to the ground. At first I thought it was just a case of hysteria, maybe drug induced psychosis."

"Are drugs a big problem away from the cities?"

"Not especially, but it does happen. I tried, but he wouldn't be calmed. The nurse who helped minister to the sick at the church's clinic couldn't calm him either. It took some effort but we carried him from the church and he finally calmed."

Friar Francis finished his own coffee and signalled the waiter for refills. They both lit another cigarette.

"Even though he seemed calmer, I heard him mumbling. Only by crouching close to him did I make any sense of it. I was surprised to hear the man reciting quotes from the Bible in Latin."

Father Moran paused while the waiter delivered their drinks.

"As you know speaking in tongues is a sign of possession, but Latin is far from a dead language. It still might have been hysteria or even a deliberate fake. However, what did catch my attention was his perfect recitation. Normally demons only quote scripture in mockery."

Friar Francis leaned forward. "Which passage?"

"Revelations chapter 6."

"An interesting choice." Friar Francis remarked.

"Yes, if a little obvious. Anyway, he passed out so we took him to the clinic and let him rest. He slept for almost the whole day before disturbing the villagers again this time with enraged shouts. In several different languages he demanded to see me. It sounded more like the bellowing of an animal. Then he called me by name. Again, not proof in itself, he may have learned my name from the locals. Still I felt convinced this was a genuine possession."

"Why?"

"Instinct I guess. When you worked with evil for so long you become attuned to it."

The Friar nodded his agreement.

"I entered the clinic; it was just a small room with a handful of metal beds. I found the nurse cowering in the corner and the young man squatting on the bed. He hadn't touched her, just bellowed for me. She was terrified, but it seemed odd."

"Demons normally enjoy some physical violence."

"Indeed. But this one wanted my attention more than gratification."

"So what did you do next?"

"I followed procedure. I checked for the four classic signs. He demonstrated each voluntarily. I've never seen such a thing before. He knew what I needed to know and provided the evidence."

"How?"

"First he pushed by me, not roughly I hasten to add. He walked outside and to the battered 4x4. He picked up the front end of the truck, not just a few inches from the ground, but clear up to his chest."

"Superhuman strength."

"Exactly and in front of witnesses. Unfortunately I didn't have a camera to hand. It would have been nice to document it properly. Next he told me of the time I first masturbated and who I fantasised about while doing it. I've never told anyone about that."

"So who was it?" The Friar asked with a smile.

"I've never told anyone and I don't intend starting now. Although it was more than a little embarrassing in front of half the village I can tell you. I should be grateful only a few spoke decent English."

The Friar chuckled.

"At this stage I was willing to take the earlier mutterings as a sign of speaking in tongues. So only the aversion to holy symbols remained. The young man, I never found out his real name, turned his back to me. I pulled a key from my pocket and touched it to the back of his neck. He flinched, but no other reaction. I repeated the action with the key. Again he didn't react. I then touched my crucifix to his neck and he howled as if I'd burned him."

"He could have been faking it."

"Possibly, but he did present the classic signs. However he then said a strange thing."

"What did he say?"

"He said he had a message about the Deathless Man."

"The Deathless Man?"

The Friar kept his face blank, but his old friend knew him too well.

"I know. It sounded familiar. I immediately thought of Lazarus. But I'd also learned about your success against that particular problem by then. I asked him if he meant Lazarus and he replied no, but the Black Friar would know. I think he meant you."

The Friar stubbed out his cigarette and immediately lit another.

"Maybe he does. What was the message?"

"He said the Black Friar would have to guide the Deathless Man. He must follow the False Gospel."

"The False Gospel? Is that a satanic text?"

His friend shook his head. "I don't think so. My best guess is he meant the Gospel of Lazarus. There are fragments in the Vatican library. I remember hearing about it during my time as a curator in the library. I've not read the text, but I've heard mention of it. It's been kept secret for years, available to Vatican scholars only. I would say it's your best place to start."

"Did the demon say anything else?"

"Not much. It said the Deathless Man is the only hope for humanity in the coming Apocalypse."

"Could this be some sort of distraction?"

"It might."

"So what happened then, did you exorcise him?"

"No, I didn't need to. He left the body. Immediately it was obvious the young man had been dead for several days."

"That must have been unpleasant."

"It was." Father Moran picked up a menu. "Shall we eat?"

Chapter 3

The first seal

Revelations chapter 6 verse 2:
And I saw, and behold a white horse: and he that sat on him had a bow; and a crown was given unto him: and he went forth conquering, and to conquer.

Pierre Roux adjusted his tie while he admired himself in the mirror. Physically he looked as if bred for politics. Although nearing sixty his face remained clear of lines except for just enough to give him a wise and trusting look. His hair contained the required smattering of grey again to cast him as a genial father or uncle. He understood exactly what he was, after all he had been tutored for this role his entire life.

He put on the jacket, expensively tailored to highlight his sleek frame. Pierre enjoyed the feel of well fitted clothes. His assistant Helen Diva walked in unannounced, the only person allowed to do so without being stopped by the guards outside the door.

"Good morning Monsieur President," she greeted him warmly.

"Not yet."

"What are a few hours? The ceremony will take place at noon."

Without Helen, Pierre wouldn't be here in the first place. All his life she had been at his side. She mentored him. She supported him. She had moulded him into the man who was about to become one of the most powerful people on the planet.

Helen's talents didn't end there. She guided the support from the many sects and organisations that existed for the sole purpose of his work. Although even she wasn't aware of the additional leverage his campaign had received. He knew all too well the source.

Even if she had known, she wouldn't have believed it.

"The Americans will be announcing their withdrawal from NATO this evening, at 11am their time."

"Finally." He smiled. It had taken years of constant secret campaigning to make the United States ever more unpopular in Europe. A similar campaign in the US turned American public opinion against the European Union. Thankfully an up swelling in support for isolationism helped push the decision through.

"As soon as they announce their departure send out the press release for the dissolution of NATO and the formation of the European Union Armed Forces." Preparations for the new pan-European force had already begun, so the announcement would come as little surprise.

"The Russians aren't going to like it."

"Of course they won't. That's the point."

"I know, but is it wise to antagonise them so soon?"

"There's nothing they can do about it and when they do, it will be too late. Besides, they still need our money to buy their oil."

"The Russian Bear isn't as toothless as we like to think," Helen warned.

"I agree, only a fool would underestimate them. However next week's ratification of Turkey joining the union will shift the balance even further in our favour. More importantly it will provide the land access we'll need in the coming months."

"Yes sir. Everything is in hand."

Naturally the negotiations had been complex. Greece had blocked the Turks admittance at every opportunity. They finally agreed to a deal only after major economic concessions had been granted in their favour.

The telephone rang. Helen answered it, speaking quickly into the handset. Pierre waited patiently for her to finish. "Well?"

"As we suspected, the Israelis have bombed the nuclear processing plant."

The nuclear processing plant had been identified by the United Nations months earlier. The EU argued against releasing the information outside the Security Council, but without success and now the Israeli Air Force had attacked the plant.

"Not unexpected, but it will alter our timing somewhat. Was the raid successful?"

"Yes. The Israelis suffered no casualties. The Iranians however are reporting hundreds of civilian dead and wounded. They're claiming the attack has released radioactive material into the air."

"Merde. Have we verified the claim?"

"Not yet, we've launched drones to verify. The Americans have done the same. The Israelis claim it hasn't. Of course there's no way of knowing if the Iranians have done it themselves to gain public support against Israel. Moscow and Beijing have already condemned the attack. It's likely the Americans will too."

"I'm surprised. I didn't think we'd have made so much progress yet." He paused and thought for a few seconds. "Of course we must express our support."

"Yes sir. I'll prepare a press statement."

"And now I have a ceremony to prepare for."

"Yes sir. You look fine."

Chapter 4

A visit from an old friend

The abyss became my refuge. The dread canyon provided my only escape from the pain stalking me. I spent so much time at the edge it might have well been my home. A more favoured home than the cold stone and tormented flesh which contained me.

So I did what any new homeowner would – I decorated.

I transformed my little area on the precipice. Creating my own personal Eden helped pass the time. The boredom ate at me almost as badly as the miracle's fire. I needed a distraction.

The pain I experienced meant I was fully aware of each passing second. Concentrating on something else helped the time slip past almost unnoticed until my will eroded and the agony flooded in once again. Besides it felt good to be occupied.

After a few false starts I picked a Parisian café as my inspiration. Why? At first I wasn't sure. I'd never been to Paris. I'd never even experienced any particular desire to go there. Maybe the fact it presented an absolute antithesis to the abyss coloured my decision.

The abyss flowed past like an obsidian seine. My little café positioned alongside provided the perfect view. I took the early 20th century as my inspiration. The clean tables and chairs were always empty.

I once conjured people to join me and a sexy waitress to serve me. The illusions only served to make the loneliness more real. I decided it was probably better to accept the desolate reality rather than create fresh torture for myself.

The abyss reacted to my presence. It boiled with anticipation, strange shapes disturbing its veil. Once, in a moment of despair, I had thrown myself in, seeking escape from my existence. Of course the miracle prevented me, refusing to allow me to pass through the membrane. But my sudden proximity had really excited the shapes beneath, their movements frantic to reach me.

That attempt occurred long ago. Now I had accepted my fate. I doubted I would ever escape. So I sat by the stygian gorge. I sipped imagined drinks and nibbled illusionary delicacies. These pretences formed my defiance of the very real hunger and thirst.

Most of all, I watched.

I watched the shapes in the abyss as they cavorted. They always reacted but they no longer made any real effort to reach me. The membrane which trapped them dampened their motion. They remained at the edge of my vision, almost hidden by the depths.

After so long I became accustomed to the distress I determined from their movements. Then one day it changed.

One of the shapes strained out of the depths. The membrane between its world and mine stretched like film. It quivered with the effort of forcing its progress. Time transformed into an elastic concept in my mind, it slowed as I watched this new occurrence. My fascination at something novel in my dull existence lifted my spirits.

As it moved closer I saw more details and suddenly I recognised him.

"Hello Lazarus."

He smiled in response.

"Bored of Hell already?"

"Not so much bored as restless, but I can see you are of yours."

His voice was muffled by the dark covering stretched tight across his face. I discerned his features, although he looked more like an animated oil slick.

"I like what you've done with the place. Very quaint."

Now I realised where the inspiration for the tableau had come from. The memories I had absorbed back when I killed him. It seemed so long ago, but was it really so distant? Somehow his memories had blended with my subconscious. The memory triggered a new worry, were my thoughts being influenced by his memories?

I considered the thought unlikely, but once you see the worm, you can't un-see it.

"I remember this very café . I was here in the 1930's. It was a bit livelier then of course. I recall a lovely young woman. I can't remember her name. Elise?"

He paused in contemplation, then with a chuckle asked: "How's the miracle treating you?" He smiled again. I'll admit the sight was a little unsettling. His lips looked black and liquid. "Hurts doesn't it? You shouldn't take what doesn't belong to you."

Lazarus didn't sound like the man I'd encountered before. The first time he'd oozed menace. The second time his mind had been confused by the drugs the Friar had pumped into him. Something in him had changed. And that bothered me.

I surged my will at him, seeking to enter his taunting head. It bounced from the membrane. Lazarus laughed as he sensed my failed attack. I remembered the Friar's teachings and took a more considered approach.

Withdrawing my will I examined the membrane itself while cursing myself for not trying this before. The membrane felt different from any shield or substance I'd encountered before. The surface felt slick, greasy and cold. I zoomed in, inspecting the structure of the substance. I saw the film wasn't uniform; instead it was constructed from countless chains. Each chain intertwined with its neighbours, a twisted helix of chains. I examined closer, looking for the imperfections as I had been taught.

"The Black Friar's tricks won't help you. This isn't a mental shield."

"So what is it?" I asked while continuing to probe. Even some conversation with a person other than me made for an interesting interlude. Besides, I still didn't understand the change in Lazarus.

"It's the veil between your reality and the one I now inhabit. You cannot cross it without dying. I on the other hand..."

"If that were true, why haven't you? I know your powers Lazarus. I now possess them. Whatever you were able to do, I can now."

"True, but you are young. I learned my powers over the span of two thousand years. How long have you possessed them?"

I'd like to know the answer to that question myself. How long had I been trapped here? I've usually been pretty good at estimating time, but with no frame of reference at all I lost track long ago.

"You don't know, do you? Well isn't this nice. Already I have something you want. I wonder what that information is worth to you."

He guessed correctly, damn him. It wouldn't do for me to show him.

"Nothing. It makes no difference how long I have been here."

"Ah, but that isn't true. I can hear the curiosity on your voice. I can smell your need. You forget I've studied your kind for centuries."

Time to change the subject.

"So what brings you here? Did you miss me so much? The last sight I had of you was as a weeping wisp being dragged into Hell."

I remembered the brief glimpse well. For only a second I had witnessed Hell, but it provided more of a surprise to me than Lazarus's vision of Heaven.

Heaven had been revealed as a paradise of community. A perfect assembly of angels who sang eternal praises to their God. Heaven's glory was evident by its absolute unity. Hell on the other hand was more confused.

I'll admit it puzzled me. Where Heaven resembled the preaching of the church to some degree, Hell presented more of an enigma.

Lazarus declined to answer, so I tried again.

"How was your stay? You enjoyed it so much you had to come and tell me about it. You could have just sent me a postcard."

Still Lazarus refused to reply, so I ignored him and continued my examination of the membrane. I failed to gain any purchase on it. The stuff which formed it was very different from anything else I had encountered.

Nor did I detect any imperfections in the chains. The gaps between the chains should have provided a natural weak point I could exploit, but they did not. The chains meshed together so perfectly they provided no gap for me to exploit. The shape of the chains should have made that impossible.

A high pitched keening broke my concentration. I looked up and saw Lazarus straining once more towards me. He wasn't looking at me; he looked more like he was moving away from something. Whatever it might be, he was far more afraid of it than of the man who ripped the miracle of eternal life from him.

A ripple in the membrane revealed another presence. Its shape lacked definition until the thing stepped from the membrane. The creature's form shimmered as it did so. He passed through the veil as if it was no more than smoke.

Tendrils of the oily film smoked into the air revealing a dapper looking young man. I was struck by his eyes of burning violence. He gestured at Lazarus's form, who now shrieked in agony. Thankfully the terrible noise lasted only a moment and then Lazarus stopped moving.

The strange man turned and faced me. He looked perfect in every respect. His skin was flawless. His suit matched the decor of my café.

"So you're the Deathless Man. I expected someone a little older." His smile didn't reach past his mouth and his voice sounded flat in an odd way.

I've never been one to shy from a challenge so I leapt straight into his mind.

And I encountered no resistance.

This wasn't the same absence I'd encountered when I first challenged Lazarus. This was different. I sensed a vastness as if his mind was too big for me to comprehend. I immediately realised he was able to prevent my invasion, but he didn't. I pulled back, realising I may have dived in a little too prematurely.

As I withdrew I caught a fragment of the shape of his mind. The scale was immense, like being lost in the desert with the flat sand stretching beyond the horizon. Lazarus had been the most complicated mind I'd entered. His was an ancient mind, powerful but still human. This majestic structure formed something far different. I tried to explore further, to gain some understanding of what this was.

A sudden supernova flared within me, the miracle reminding me I existed only by its tender mercies. The pain wrenched me from the visitor's mind. My oasis by the abyss faded and then snapped back into being as the stranger touched me.

I'd never experienced the miracle so easily thwarted.

"Who are you?"

"I have many names, but you can call me Venet."

He sat in one of the empty chairs.

"How can you pass through the veil?"

"The skill comes with my vocation."

"Your vocation?"

"I'm a hunter. I catch the little fish that jump the fence." He gestured at Lazarus again who popped and disappeared. "And those that try to."

"What are you?"

I know. It's a little rude to just come out with the question like that. In my defence I've been trapped inside myself for an eternity. My social graces were a little lacking. Anyway, he didn't seem to mind.

"You'd probably call me a demon. You'd be wrong but after thousands of years of propaganda it's an understandable mistake."

"A demon?" OK, I was a little surprised. I shouldn't be after all I'd seen so far.

He signed. "No not really. Anyway, I have souls to catch. I'll see you again. Soon."

And on that dramatic note, he vanished.

Chapter 5

The hunter returns

The pain returned the moment Venet disappeared. Having been held at bay the miracle came back with a vengeance. My will proved insufficient to block the pain it forced me to suffer in my ruined body. As always only the faint chants of the monks kept me company.

Even when the pain faded I needed more effort than ever before to return to my sanctuary. When I finally did, it didn't feel the same. My tableau now felt emptier somehow. The brief contact with somebody else, even Lazarus reminded me of how alone I truly was.

It's not a problem which ever bothered me before. I'd always been surrounded by other people, even if they only existed for me to raid their memories and thoughts. Here there was nobody. I discovered how boring life is without anyone to torment. Or even converse with.

I sat at the table and gazed into the abyss.

A pop in the air announced the visitor. Venet returned, this time wearing a more casual linen suit.

"Welcome to my café," I greeted him. "Would you care for any refreshment?"

He sat in the chair opposite me. He offered me a lopsided smile.

"No but let me offer you some."

A gesture with his manicured hand and a glass appeared on the table. Looking at the glass and its contents I knew it was real. My throat ached to feel the water's cool caress. I restrained my eagerness and sipped from the glass. The water tasted sublime. Honey couldn't have tasted any sweeter. With great control I sipped again, and placed the glass down.

"How is that possible?"

If I learnt that trick it would ease a lot of my suffering.

"A reasonable question," Venet answered. "Outside of my own reality I have more control over the experiences of its inhabitants. It helps we are in your own reality."

"How?"

"It's easier because there is only you I need to convince the change was real."

"So the drink was an illusion after all?"

"In a way. But an illusion which fooled even the physical thirst you suffer."

I considered the conundrum for a moment then discarded the question. I could examine the mystery later at my leisure.

"How is Lazarus?"

"Back where he belongs. Most people have a choice for their afterlife. He's one of the lucky ones who have the choice made for them."

Another surprise. "People get a choice? Do you mean by the lives they live?"

"No, although how they live their lives shapes their choice."

"What do you mean?"

"Well if you live a life of selfless devotion, to God or the world around you, then your path naturally inclines you towards Heaven. So when you make the choice that will be your decision."

"I see."

"You don't." Another cold smile. "But you will when the time comes."

"So Lazarus is condemned to Hell?"

"Yes and when he tries to escape it's my job to bring him back."

"Does he escape often?"

"He tries, but the next attempt will be a bit difficult for him."

"Why?"

"Let's just say he's been divided into several pieces and is now visiting some of the more interesting parts of my master's domain."

I enjoyed the understatement and the thought of Lazarus's torment. Hey, he tortured me first. I then turned my mind to more immediate matters.

"That trick with the water. Does that mean you can help me get out of here?"

I'm not so much of an optimist that I expected a favourable answer, but I had to ask just in case.

"No. Entering the reality inside your head I can do without notice. To free you from your bonds requires physical intervention."

"Isn't entering my mind the same as entering my reality?"

"Not quite. Your mind creates its own reality, in parallel to the physical one your body inhabits. We can enter human minds without restriction, but the physical reality you inhabit isn't so easy."

"Why?"

"The main problem is the limited nature of your physical reality. You see it's difficult for us to squeeze into the reduced dimensions. Your minds don't suffer the same limitations."

"You said 'the main problem'. What are the other reasons?"

"Over time we discovered certain proscriptions which controlled our access to your universe. Although the usual rules appear to be entering a state of flux."

"What do you mean?"

"That I can't tell you, not yet anyway."

"So you can't help me?"

"Not in the way you want, but I can make your circumstances a little easier."

"How so?"

"Would you like another drink?"

"OK, point taken. So Hell isn't just a place of punishment?"

"It was. Still is to an extent. However Hell is more than the lakes of fire described in religious texts. "

He conjured a cigarette from the air, then another for me. Damn it tasted good.

"To make you understand I suppose I should tell you the story from the beginning."

Chapter 6

The great rebellion

After inhaling from the cigarette, Venet opened with a question.

"Do you know what an angel is?"

I shrugged. "Not really. A being of spirit created by God?"

"Well that's true of everything in a sense, including you. Or more correctly, everything is God."

"I'm not sure I understand."

"Think of the universe. In a way you are a creation of the universe as well as a part of it. Understand?"

"Sure."

"It's the same with God. He is everything that exists."

Sometimes it would be nice to go back to a time when I didn't have to know about any of this. Back to a simpler time when there was only me and my victims.

"All right, so God created you. Why?"

"Again created isn't quite the right term. It's more like God expressed us. I wasn't part of the first founding, that honour belongs to the archangels like Michael and Gabriel."

"And Lucifer?"

"Yes. He was the first amongst us. With hindsight that was probably significant."

"In what way?"

"We'll get to that."

More damn mystery. Friars, angels, none of them give you a straight answer.

"All right, why did God create you?"

"A good question." Patronising too. "As with any intelligent entity God was lonely. Unfortunately for him no other gods existed for him to interact with. He is everything which exists and he has no external frame of reference."

"Are you saying we're all in God's head?"

"In a way. His thoughts expressed us."

"So is that what angels are? God's thoughts?"

"Again the analogy isn't exact, but it's close enough. The first angels represented the primal aspects of God. As his understanding of himself grew, so did the comprehension of the first foundlings. As more aspects unfolded new angels came into being."

"Like yourself?"

"Indeed."

"So what happened?"

"Although angels represent a particular aspect, they became more than the initial spark. But the aspect remains core to their being. As the first angel Lucifer represented God's individuality, his desire to be."

"I think I can see where this is heading."

"The story has been told many times and there's even some truth to them. For an age unmeasured we dwelt together. In communion we continued the construction of Heaven. We built a paradise of such symmetrical perfection the memory haunts me even now. We were all in harmony, working together as brothers."

"I suppose we all know the happy families didn't last, so what happened?"

"As it is with God the whole of what we are is reflected in our form. Not the disguise I currently wear, but my true form. As we develop our form becomes ever more complicated, this also makes us completely readable to each other. At a glance we know what another angel is thinking, or even what they have been thinking. Angels cannot keep secrets from other angels. That remains true even now with many of us fallen."

"What about when you are disguised?"

"A surface illusion like this makes no difference. When we are on your world and wearing a skin suit we become harder to read. We have the same skills as you, with a bit more power. That's balanced by the fact we can conceal our thoughts better than most humans."

"So Lucifer started acting differently?"

"He did. We built Heaven together with a shared vision and unified purpose. After a time he started to add flourishes which didn't match the common vision."

Venet paused, conjured refreshments of cool water and breaded snacks.

"If Lucifer was the most independent of us then Michael was the most conformist. Michael represented the status quo. God's need for consistency."

"So Michael didn't approve of Lucifer's changes to Heaven?"

"He didn't. At first the contention occurred only between them as individuals. All too quickly the argument escalated and other angels started taking sides. The arguments began to occupy more time and effort than the building. The wasted time enraged Michael even further."

"Why did God allow this division?"

Venet sighed. It sounded both a vexed and mournful, a stark contrast from his usual demeanour of thinly veiled condescension.

"Another good question. Each angel represents a different aspect of God. Only with consensus can we assume to know God's will. As such we represent his state of being; some of us think this conflict represents confusion in him."

"How can that be?"

"Think of it this way. Imagine being born with a mind already self-aware. Now consider if your mind existed in absolute isolation. You experience no external input; all that exists is your mind. Your mind is the reality in which you exist."

I drank more of the delicious water. "I think I see the problem. You are all in his head."

"It's a simplistic analogy, but it will suffice for now."

I wondered where all this was heading, not that it really mattered. I've always been a sucker for a good story.

"Did he not communicate with you?"

"In ways. Mysterious ways you might say." Another cold smile favoured me.

"What ways?"

"God had been building Heaven long before angels appeared. Even as they combined their efforts God continued to shape creation with us. Perhaps most telling was he didn't alter or destroy the creations of Lucifer or his allies."

"And the lack of response spurred Lucifer on, didn't it?"

"It did and it angered Michael greatly. Eventually the conflict encompassed the whole of both factions. Unfortunately for us, the independents were greatly outnumbered by Michael's cohorts."

"So Michael forced you out of Heaven?"

"Not quite. The conflict came to violence, the first of such known to God. The first battle also witnessed the first deaths of angels. I think the deaths shocked God into action."

I leaned forward. "What did he do?"

"God split Heaven into three, unequal parts. In the smallest part he sent Lucifer and his angels. One moment we battled against Michael's army, the next we were far away."

"He cast you into Hell?"

"Hell is a pejorative term, much like demon. We are still angels. As I said before, we're not demons. Demons are something else."

"So what are they?"

"They are a different part of the story. Gradually parts of Hell have become like the descriptions in literature, but that was by necessity rather than divine dictate. Between Michael's Heaven and Lucifer's Hell

God created a vast chasm. He created a void which stretched almost for eternity. His goal was simply to separate the warring factions until unity could be restored."

I've seen Heaven. Unity wouldn't have been my favoured choice.

Chapter 7

Gospel of Lazarus

Friar Francis examined the high resolution scans of the manuscript fragments. The actual manuscript was kept in permanent storage for its protection. The slightest rustle of air might irreparably damage the fragments.

The Friar discovered that the text had been declared for restricted access only. Before reading the text itself he checked the access log. The file had only been accessed three times. The first entry was dated over ten years ago when the artefact had first been scanned. The second was much more recently, in fact only a week ago by Bishop Gabaldi.

The Friar recognised the name. The Bishop was a member of the Swiss Guard, the principal liaison with the Holy Inquisition. He thought it odd the Inquisition had suddenly taken an interest in this text.

Next he read through the notes from previous scholars who researched the text when first discovered during an archaeological dig in Iraq. Only two readable fragments had been recovered. Although neither mentioned Lazarus by name the text did refer to the Deathless Man. While other immortals were known in the world the scholars unanimously assumed the manuscript referred to Lazarus.

Reading the passages for himself, Friar Francis wasn't as convinced. The first fragment spoke of the life of the Deathless Man. The stilted verse mentioned a trauma early in the man's life. The pages also described the evil the man perpetrated throughout his early years.

It's possible the text applied to Lazarus, but if it did then why didn't the text include his time in ministry with Christ? Another glaring omission had been the resurrection. An almost unique occurrence in history, yet no mention of the event was included in the text.

The scholars had noted the text had large gaps in the narrative. They used these holes to bolster their theory.

Friar Francis considered this sloppy thinking. Reading the fragments he didn't think the text was about Lazarus at all. But they did fit somebody imprisoned in a monastery wall in the baked mountains of Cyprus. A person the Friar had hidden from the world, for the world's safety. That made reading the second fragment all the more disturbing.

"Excuse me, Friar."

The soft voice disturbed the Friar's thoughts. He looked up to see an elderly monk, one of the many librarians here.

"There is a telephone call for you."

The librarian frowned as he spoke.

The Friar thanked him and followed the monk to the main desk. He picked up the old fashioned phone.

"Hello."

The line was silent. He turned to the monk.

"Who was it?"

"I'm sorry. He didn't say."

Replacing the handset in its cradle the Friar returned to the desk. The librarian returned to his newspaper rereading the headlines of the latest world tensions. He didn't notice that his notes lay in a different position to how he left them as he continued studying the first fragment.

He spent most of the day piecing together the words, trying to gain some further understanding. As the light from the windows dimmed he decided to leave studying the second fragment until the next day, come back at it with a fresh mind after some rest. He already had a rough notion from the previous scholars' notes of what the fragment contained. The pages spoke of the role the Deathless Man would play in the end days. A role which didn't quite fit the evil the man had known through his whole life.

Here was a paradox to be studied on another day. The Friar wearily rose from the chair and exited the library. He didn't notice the monk who had spent the whole day watching him, as Friar Francis picked up the telephone and dialled an internal number.

When Friar Francis returned the next day, the Gospel of Lazarus was no longer available in the library archive.

Chapter 8

The second seal

Revelation chapter 6 verse 4:
And there went out another horse that was red: and power was given to him that sat thereon to take peace from the earth, and that they should kill one another: and there was given unto him a great sword.

"The Russian and Chinese ambassadors have both presented complaints to our Foreign Minister," Helen said the moment she entered the office. This office looked much grander than Pierre's previous office as a lowly Member of the European Parliament. The role suited him.

"And good morning to you Helen. I hope the good minister was suitably dismissive of the complaint. After all they are both supplying weapons to Iran."

"He was, but they'll keep pushing. Hostilities between Iran and Israel have been increasing steadily since the air strike. The rocket attacks from Lebanon and Gaza mysteriously stopped a few days ago. At first we assumed the success of the Iron Dome system in shooting down the missiles forced them to give up. It turned out they were stockpiling for a massive assault."

"Were they successful?"

"Yes sir. They fired thousands of smaller rockets to overwhelm the tracking system and then fired larger missiles. Those larger weapons were definitely not homemade."

"Iran?"

"Yes. Iron Dome actually performed well considering. The system shot down 99% of the incoming rockets the computers determined as likely to land in occupied regions. The last few got through mainly because of lack of ammunition."

"Where there many casualties?"

"Some. So far only a dozen deaths have been confirmed, but the injured are in their thousands."

Pierre nodded, his satisfaction at the turn of events evident on his face.

"And the Israeli retaliation?"

"Drone strikes have already started in Gaza. Satellite intelligence reports Israeli air assets scrambling from all major airbases. The generals think they're going to strike targets inside Iran."

"This could get messy." Pierre sounded pleased at the thought.

"Yes sir. It might."

"Good. It's earlier than we planned, but we need to take advantage."

"What about the army sir? They won't be ready on this timescale."

"The Turks can handle any immediate threats. Focus on the units which act as a force multiplier. Artillery, special forces and air units. Start moving them to the border."

"I'll get on it sir," Helen replied. "We've also received a message from the United Nations Secretary General."

"And what does that old windbag want?"

"He wants to arrange peace talks. They'll mediate, but also want us to act as guarantors."

"Do they now?" Pierre rose from his desk, opened the window and lit a cigarette. Helen coughed disapprovingly. He chuckled. "You know these things can't harm me."

"No sir, but they can harm your image."

"There's only you here. Now let me think for a moment."

He smoked slowly, finishing his cigarette before speaking again.

"Tell the UN we'll gladly support their peace process as soon as Iran stops attacking Israel through its proxy terrorists. China and Russia must also stop their weapons supply shipments. Make sure the statement is made public."

"Of course. We've made arrangements for you to attend a charity dinner at the old abbey. It's a small private occasion and the building has a suitably prepared basement."

As President it was difficult to maintain the proper ceremonies, but thanks to Helen suitable arrangements were made.

"Excellent, it's been too long since I enjoyed a rare vintage. Oh and tell the Israeli ambassador we support him fully."

Chapter 9

True demons

Venet left me to my own devices for what I guessed to be several days. I'm not really sure how much time had passed. I suppose I should have been used to the loneliness by then. No matter the actual time, it felt far too long.

The thirst and hunger returned. I thought about what Venet had told me. Some things didn't make sense and I wanted to know more. Mulling the information over at least gave me something else to ponder. I also continued to probe at the membrane. I didn't really learn anything, but the attempt occupied the time.

The soft pop in the air heralded Venet's arrival. This time he wore a black formal suit. Without request he created drinks and food on the table. With a mumbled greeting I dived straight in. He sat and watched me.

"I thought you'd be back sooner," I complained, hating the sound of my weakness.

"I'm not at your beck and call."

"You promised to make my time here better."

Again that whining tone in my voice.

"And I will, but I have other matters that require my attention."

"Lazarus again?"

"Unfortunately so. I don't know how he managed to reassemble himself, but he did. That man has been full of surprises for too many years. And now I have to track him down again. I hoped he would be here again."

"Sorry, I haven't seen him."

"I'm sure he'll visit soon, he hates you a lot."

I had no argument against that. "Do you have time for some questions?"

"I can spare some time, what's on your mind?"

"I've been thinking about what you told me. And two things keep bothering me. The first is why Lucifer rebelled. It doesn't make sense for God's independence and his need for stability to be so at odds."

"You said two things, what was the second?"

"Demons. You said you are a fallen angel, and that demons are something different. What did you mean?"

"I find it interesting you picked up those two points. Maybe you're smarter than I thought."

I let that pass for now. His superiority annoyed me, but until I learned that trick of his there was nothing to be done. My time would come.

"Why?"

"The two are connected."

I watched the glossy shapes in the depths twist through each other. I supposed instinctively I grasped there had to be a connection.

"How are they connected?"

"The word demon is normally meant to represent a denizen of Hell. This isn't quite the case. All angels, fallen or otherwise remain angels. Demons are very different."

Venet drank some water before continuing. "Even after all this time, we still don't know exactly what demons are. Our best guess is they are entities not part of God."

"How can they be separate from God? Isn't God everything?"

"He is, but somehow these beings are different. They aren't part of God like angels are. They're also not a consequence of a specific reality like humans."

With that statement he added another puzzle, but it could wait for now.

"So what are they?"

"As I said we don't know. You can't imagine how frustrating it is for beings who know everything. We believe God doesn't perceive them and they cannot interact directly with God's creation."

"What do you mean they can't interact with God's creation?"

"Exactly what I said. Where angels can modify Heaven and everything within, demons cannot. They can communicate, but not directly influence."

"What does this have to do with Lucifer?"

"Angels have an in-built connection; we know each other as soon as we encounter another. The demons first appeared soon after the first founding. There were never very many of them. Now there's none at all."

"Why?"

"We exterminated them."

"Seems a little harsh," I joked.

"We had to. They were a threat, to both sides. One of the few things Michael and Lucifer cooperated on was the hunting down of these demons. In fact, that was how I became a hunter in the first place."

"So what happened?"

"At first we ignored the demons. That proved to be a big mistake. We let them mingle amongst us as we shaped Heaven. They didn't interfere with our work and appeared content to just observe.

"Gradually they began interacting with us. For the most part they focused on the archangels. Most angels ignored them, some like Michael dismissed them. In Lucifer they gained an audience. His thirst for new knowledge probably caused his fall."

"Did you interact with the demons?"

"To my everlasting sorrow I did."

"Why sorrow?"

"It's difficult to explain. We were beings in complete union with God and each other. The fall changed all that. It broke the connection between us."

"But you gained from the change as well?"

He nodded. "An astute observation. Yes we did, to an extent. Whether you're correct is open to debate, but yes the contact with these demons broadened our horizons, and gave us new ways of thinking."

"Did all of the fallen angels have contact with these demons?"

"Most, but not all. Some were changed by the angels who had already chosen their side. The fall had another impact. Up until then new angels were still being created. After we were seperated no further angels were created."

"Why not?"

"We don't know. I've listened to many theories. Maybe God thought we were a flawed creation. Or maybe he decided he needed to fix us before creating anymore."

I wondered, how you fixed an angel?

Chapter 10

A fair faced visitor

We sat and drank in silence for a while. A sudden voice surprised me, Venet didn't appear as shocked at the disembodied speech.

"Being maudlin again? Venet you need to take a lighter perspective on things."

This new being looked more obviously an angel, her face fair in a way no mortal's could ever be. From her pale skin a luminescence softened the stark lines of the abyss. Her smile radiated warmth in a way I could never have imagined. She bore no wings, and she appeared naked, although her form was shrouded in the glow.

A bit small for my tastes, but I won't deny a little stirring in the trouser region.

"Hemal, nice of you to join us."

So they know each other. Wonderful, although he didn't sound that happy to see her.

Hemal, to me the name sounded too clunky for this divine apparition. I thought of all the women I'd ever known. None of them were a match for this ethereal creature.

"Venet, he's having naughty thoughts about me," she teased.

"Well cloth yourself, or maybe show him your true form, that'll dampen his spirits."

"You're not an angel?" I felt a little disappointed.

"Oh she's an angel all right. But so am I. How many times do I have to tell you that? We can appear as we like and she loves to tease. Although teasing a man locked in his own body isn't any challenge in my opinion."

Hemal pouted at him.

Venet ignored her and continued. "And if you're trying to ask whether she's a fallen angel, then no she's not."

"So what do you mean true form? I know these aren't your real bodies, but are your true forms so horrific?"

"Not at all." Her voice contained a husky quality, although still light with amusement. "Just way beyond your comprehension."

"I don't know what you mean."

Venet snorted as if my words confirmed his opinion of my intellect.

Hemal settled into the seat beside me. Her scent overwhelmed my senses.

"In our natural form we are almost geometric in nature. But those geometries are impossible to comprehend in this limited universe. We occupy dimensions beyond counting meaning we are able to express ourselves by growing in any way we please."

Venet interrupted. "We are not bound by physical convention in the same way you people are in this universe. In Heaven there is no physicality. We have no limits to how we can manipulate ourselves and the space around us."

I nodded. "To you dimensions work the same as for our mathematicians?"

"In a way." He turned to Hemal. "It's always nice to see you, but what brings you here?"

It was my turn to interrupt. "Wait a minute. You said she's not a fallen angel, so presumably she's working for Michael's side?"

"I am a member of Michael's legions, but the situation is a little more complicated than..."

Venet spoke before she continued and I noticed the sharp look he threw her.

"There's always been individual contact between members of the two factions. Some of us have always hoped for reconciliation."

"How's that working out?"

Again they shared a look.

"Are you two going to tell me what is going on?"

Hemal answered. "The final battle is coming."

"How? I stopped Lazarus."

"It's not Lazarus. This is more serious."

Of course it was. I sighed. "And what has this got to do with me?"

"You're the Deathless Man."

"Much good that is doing me," I retorted. "I'm basically living in my own personal Hell, trapped within my flesh in eternal agony."

This time Venet answered. "That isn't the issue right now."

"It is for me!"

"I understand and when the time comes you'll be released."

"If you can release me then why not do so now?"

"We can't release you and to do so would be dangerous anyway."

"Why?"

"They're looking for you."

"Who's looking for me?"

"We're working on finding out. All we can tell you is that the first two seals have been broken. The seals signify the approach of the Apocalypse."

An oh so familiar story.

"What does this have to do with me?"

"We're still finding out," Venet answered. "I wish it had nothing to do with you. We know of elements in both factions who are working together to bring about the final battle."

"All right, keep your secrets. Why now?"

"The simple answer is humans. Both sides see you and your kind as a threat to the status quo."

Chapter 11

All on the same side

Father Francis had endured a frustrating week. The curators of the Vatican Library failed to find the Gospel of Lazarus, either the original or the digital replica. He checked with the librarians of his order in case they had a copy. They reported theirs had disappeared as well. Further checking discovered all the research on the text had also been erased. So far no trace had been found.

He'd even tried some contacts in the Curate, only to find them busy with the latest European politics. For the past decade the Vatican had established a good working relationship with the European Union and an even longer history with individual countries.

The Friar turned to the only possible source left, the Internet. The problem wasn't finding information; it was separating the useful information from the pages and pages of useless ramblings. So he spent the weekend in his tiny office trying to find something to work with. The search proved a wasted effort and he was still in the office when the sun rose on Monday morning.

He cursed at the monitors which displayed another rambling website full of half truths and delusional fantasy. His head ached from eye strain and lack of sleep. The thought of another cup of coffee made him feel a little nauseous. Drained of energy he decided to take a short nap in the office.

His eyes barely closed when the door opened. Opening them again while trying to think good thoughts he saw a stocky bishop filling the door frame. A moment passed before the Friar dragged recognition from his exhausted mind.

"Bishop Gabaldi." Friar Francis rose to greet the unexpected visitor. "How can I be of assistance your Eminence?"

"Please sit, Friar. I'm sorry to disturb your repose."

The Friar thought he detected a hint of reproach in the Bishop's voice.

"Sorry your eminence, I've been here all weekend. I guess the strain finally caught up with me."

"I understand. I've pulled more than a few all day and night operations with the guard."

The comment sparked a memory in the Friar's head. Bishop Gabaldi had started as a trooper in the Swiss Guard. He served for fifteen years before taking the cloth. Now twelve years later he had risen to become a Bishop. The first Swiss Guard trooper to have managed the feat for centuries.

Gabaldi had a reputation for being smart and efficient.

"Can I offer you refreshment your eminence?"

"That won't be necessary Friar."

When they'd both sat the Bishop leaned forward.

"I have a matter of some delicacy I need to discuss with you."

"How can I help?"

"The business last year with Lazarus. You did well dealing with him."

"Thank you, your eminence."

"Some of my boys were on the operation. They said it was one of the best actions they took part in."

Those words immediately put the Friar on alert. Gabaldi might have been their old boss, but the troopers would never talk about an operation as secret as that one had been.

"I'm sorry your eminence. I'm not allowed to discuss it."

The Bishop frowned. "Of course, I understand. Ordinarily I wouldn't even ask, but this is a matter of urgency."

"What matter?"

"Now I'm the one who has to be reticent. The problem isn't within your area of expertise."

"Then I'm sorry, I don't see how I can help."

The Bishop looked the Friar in the eye.

"We have a dilemma. I can see I'm going to have to trust you. I hope you can be discreet?"

"Of course."

"The other side are making their move. The second seal has already been broken so we are running out of time."

"How does this concern Lazarus?"

"It doesn't. My visit concerns the asset you used to take care of Lazarus."

More alarm bells rang. Only the head of the order and the office of the Holy See had been told about the prisoner in the monastery wall who'd taken down Lazarus.

"Can you tell me why?"

The Bishop hesitated, but the Friar was now alert enough to see it was an act. Gabaldi was trying to play him.

"The Deathless Man is vital for Satan's plan. They are looking for him. We have to find him before they do."

"The Deathless Man?"

The Bishop showed a flash of anger before suppressing it.

"You know who the Deathless Man is as well as I do Friar. You've been researching him in the library and online."

"Why do they need him?"

"We're not sure. We've received some intelligence they are looking for him. We need your help finding him. I can't emphasise how important it is for us to get to him first."

"I'm not sure what you want from me?"

The Bishop shook his head.

"You know precisely what I want. The man in your employ who stole Lazarus's miracle. Now tell me where he is."

"I'm sorry, your eminence. I can't tell you any information without the express approval of the Holy See."

The Bishop rose, hiding his anger poorly.

"Then I'll go to the office and get the authorisation. Your refusal to help has been noted."

Friar Francis waited for him to leave. Then rose and walked to the window. He watched the Bishop stride across the quiet road. He noticed a lone figure, partially obscured by a road sign. The man watched the Bishop walk away and then turned to look at the window.

Chapter 12

Guard duty

Officer Hammond paced along the corridor. This early in the morning all was still quiet. He liked this time of day. Almost everybody was asleep, even his partner officer snoozed in the wing office. Only his measured footsteps broke the silence. In another hour the day shift would arrive and the sky would lighten and the fragile peace would be destroyed for another day.

He had slipped back into the routine of prison life easily. The job felt comfortable, yet somehow lacking. The operation in Cyprus against Lazarus had resurrected a spark he thought long dead.

Not since his tours of Iraq and Afghanistan had he experienced such a thrill. No thrill wasn't the right word. He felt pride from utilising the skills that came naturally to him. Hammond knew pride was a sin, but was not using the talents God gave you also a sin?

After the debriefing he volunteered to stay with the team.

The Friar tried to keep him assigned, but the Order had overruled him. They wanted him to return to his life as a Prison Officer. He didn't like it, but he did know how to obey orders. So here he was, patrolling the familiar corridors. His fellow officers mocked his tan and the convicts secretly admired it.

Officially he still served in the reserves for the Royal Marines. So that had been the cover story for his absence.

Lost in thoughts of what had been, he almost missed the noise. A muffled exclamation followed by the sound of a soft body falling to the floor. Hammond stopped, twisted his head trying to pinpoint the noise. All of a sudden the silence felt oppressive. He heard nothing further.

The smell led him to the cell door. He opened the flap and looked inside. He didn't see anything lurking in the shadows. The copper scent was familiar. The smell identified what he would see when he switched on the light.

Blood. Crimson and glistening was the first thing he saw.

The still body was the second. The inmate, Hammond struggled to remember his name, lay still on the floor. A pool of his blood glistened beneath him.

Hammond hit the emergency alarm.

"Wing D, cell 14. Inmate down, probable suicide."

"Confirmed. Response team on their way."

Waiting for the response team wasn't an option. Protocol dictated he should wait, but the man would definitely be dead if he did. Hammond's keys sounded loud in the pre-dawn stillness. The lock when it snapped open sounded even louder. He heard some stirring and grumbling from the neighbouring cells. He pushed the door open and almost slipped on the blood as he rushed in.

Kneeling in the blood he checked the pulse of the fallen inmate. The pulse was weak and fading fast. The inmate opened his eyes and tried to speak.

"Don't talk. Help is on its way." Hammond told him.

Hammond checked the inmate's body. Deep lacerations covered his arms and neck. The blood at his neck bubbled as he weakly breathed in and out. He reached out and grabbed a towel then pressed it against the wounds on the throat.

The inmate tried to push Hammond away. Even without being on death's door he wouldn't have stood a chance against Hammond's bulk.

"The Deathless Man," the dying man whispered.

"Don't talk, help is coming."

"No. The choice was mine."

"This isn't the way. Work with me here. You don't have to die today."

The inmate smiled.

"This is what I want. You have to warn him."

"Warn who?"

"The Deathless Man."

"Why?"

Hammond felt the man's life escape, there would be no further answers. He comprehended instantly who the dying words referred to, but didn't know why. The Friar would know.

Unfortunately it would be some time before he'd have the opportunity to contact the Friar. All calls from the prison were routinely monitored. That included calls from staff as well as the inmates. The preliminary investigation into the suicide would take place before he finished his shift.

Before starting the paperwork Hammond was allowed to shower and change. As he stood in the hot shower watching the blood sluice from his body he remembered the other casualties he had seen. Soldiers, civilians and prisoners. No matter the cause, or the victim the blood was always the same.

In the wing office he completed the required forms then in curiosity retrieved the prisoner's file on the computer. He saw nothing unusual in the file, certainly no indications Matt Jenkins was a suicide risk. He'd been in and out of prison several times in his thirty years. He was used to life inside the prison walls. He wasn't a known troublemaker and rarely had any problems with the other convicts.

Scrolling through the file Hammond checked the convictions record. Small time stuff for the most part. Some robbery, burglary, a few fights, and the latest conviction for street robbery. He scanned back up to the personal details. No next of kin, that was unusual. Hammond spotted another oddity in the religion section. Prisoners often chose Satanism just to try and mess with the system. A weak form of rebellion. To choose 'The Left Hand Path' sounded more authentic. Another question Hammond hoped the Friar could answer.

Four hours later after the compulsory interviews and counselling offers Hammond left the prison. The sun hung high and warm in the sky. He drove into town rather than back home. Some instinct warned him of something larger at play. He would call the Friar from a payphone nowhere near his home.

After parking he wandered back and forth through the town centre making sure he wasn't being followed. The trained paranoia sparked old instincts within him. It felt good to be back in action again. He was tired from the extended shift, but the hint of intrigue pushed the weariness into the background. Finally satisfied he wasn't being observed he rang the Friar.

Two minutes later he made a second call, this one to book a flight to Rome.

Chapter 13

The third seal

Revelations chapter 6 verse 6
And I heard a voice in the midst of the four beasts say, A measure of wheat for a penny, and three measures of barley for a penny; and [see] thou hurt not the oil and the wine.

The President of the European Union chuckled as he read the doom laden headlines on his tablet. The thought excited Pierre to think how the news feeds would react as the horrors increased as he was sure they would.

The war between Israel and Iran escalated into a land conflict. The Israelis fought off the Iranian attacks, although they now relied on European air power to support their ground war. Thanks to Helen Diva's secret diplomacy, he expected the Arab Gulf States would soon join the campaign against Iran. The alliance would further ignite the conflict in the Persian Gulf and oil prices would double almost overnight.

Pierre planned to earn an enormous profit from the chaos. The Chinese and Russians openly backed their ally. The Chinese had depended on Iran for its oil for years. They'd openly ignored UN sanctions to obtain it.

For the Russians, Iran ranked as their second largest client for arms, paid for with Chinese money. The US still attempted to remain neutral, but losing a few oil tankers would spur them into action.

A discrete tone from his phone reminded him of his next meeting. His smile slipped. Everything so far had proceeded as planned, but still people tried to prevent the inevitable. Two of those people now waited impatiently outside. He cast his mind out through the wall and delved into their thoughts. He cast a thought to one of the guards and sat up to await the unwelcome guests.

The guard responded to the thought command and admitted the two ministers. Pierre rose to greet them. "Minister Crowley." They shook hands. Richard Crowley was a genuine English Lord. Now he was the Finance Minister for the European Union.

His companion Hans Leder also greeted the President. He was the Minister for Social Care. Both had been working together to formulate a plan to tackle the rising social problems across Europe and provide aid for the raging famine in Africa. As had proved to be the case many times before, the relief effort was hampered by the unrest in the region.

"Please sit. Both of you. Would you care for some refreshments?"

They both did as they were bid and sat, then declined the offer of drinks. Pierre sensed their disquiet in his presence. As his power increased with each broken seal he needed to devote more attention to preventing his true essence spilling out. Even the most prosaic of people sensed the dark aura. He fixed his best smile to dispel their unease.

"Ministers, I appreciate you have both been working hard. Have you found solutions for our problems?"

"Mr President, our real problem is the escalating conflict between Israel and Iran," the Finance Minister said. "It's costing the union a fortune."

Pierre smiled, but took care not to allow it to reach his face. That was partly what the war was for. Even more importantly, the conflict would be a drain on all of the world's major economies.

The sudden cost had already delayed a co-ordinated response to the various famines in East and Central Africa. Rising oil prices also caused spiralling food prices across the world. Millions of people were already going hungry. In a few months the number would spike and without the support of the developed countries the United Nations lacked the resources and support to stop it.

"I understand completely, Lord Crowley."

The two ministers were the only members of his cabinet who weren't personal supporters. Political expediency forced him into including them in his cabinet, but they had since proved a constant irritation. In moments like this he liked to imagine them stretched side by side on a blasphemous altar.

They both looked startled for a second as if catching a glimpse of his fantasy. Pierre clamped down his restraint and turned his mind to the matter at hand. He forced his aura to emanate warmth and trust. The same power he'd used over the years to sway voters to his will.

"I'm not sure you do, Herr President." The Minister for Social Care spoke this time. "We're seeing rising social unrest across Europe. With rising inflation and more of the budget being diverted to support the combat operations we're struggling to address the key problems."

Pierre allowed the reptilian smile reach his face.

"And who are causing the problems?"

"Mr President the Iranians aren't a threat to us. We don't need a full mobilisation along the border. Combined with the cost of unifying all the national militaries, it's bleeding the treasury dry."

"We will not abandon Israel like the Americans have," Pierre turned to Hans Leder. "And you have not answered my question. Who is causing trouble? The police report states the immigrants are the source."

"The trouble is in the poor areas, they're the ones being hit hardest with the economic troubles."

"So it's not the immigrants?"

Again Crowley tried to intercede, but Pierre immediately cut him off.

"Ministers, I thank you both for your time, but this seems like a police matter. "

The Internal Security Minister had been ordained in the President's blood; he could be trusted to do exactly what was needed. It's never wise to fight a war on two fronts, but if you didn't need to win the war then it would be a lot of fun.

As they left he used his thoughts to calm the two ministers' minds. By the time they reached their offices they were convinced that the President was of the same mind as them.

Chapter 14

Let there be light

"Why are humans such a threat?"

It seemed a reasonable question to me, but both Venet and Hemal took their time in answering. I stood up and gazed down into the abyss and watched the rolling shapes below while I waited. Venet broke the silence first.

"The universe was created for a specific purpose and after billions of years it appeared humans are to be the fruition of that purpose."

"So God did create the universe?" After all I had seen this still surprised me.

"I've already told you that God is everything. So yes God created the universe, but not in the way you think. He caused the universe to come into being."

That made no sense. "What's the difference?"

Venet frowned and Hemal interjected.

"God didn't create the universe in the sense that he built it from nothing. Naturally he had the option of following that course. The universe is a part of God's being, so he could have built the cosmos in the same way we built Heaven. "

"So why didn't he?"

"That would have defeated the purpose of its creation."

"Its purpose? Why was the universe created?"

"It all stemmed from Lucifer's fall and the forced separation between Lucifer and Michael. God created a vast void between the factions. The void didn't keep them apart for long."

"So the war continued?"

"Yes, although war is probably too strong a word. There wasn't massed conflict, not at that point, but both sides skirmished against each other. God wanted to find a way to resolve and end the conflict."

I drained a glass of the chilled water. I still didn't know how they created food and drink which actually sustained me, but I wasn't going to complain. One aspect of all this puzzled me. OK more accurately, one point amongst many others, puzzled me.

"Why did God go to all this trouble?"

"What do you mean?"

"Well, why didn't God recreate you? The problem would go away."

"We're all an aspect of God. Changing us wouldn't fix the problem; it would only change how the problem is manifested."

I wondered if God had indeed tried what I suggested. I doubted whether the angels would know if it had happened.

"OK, so God is trying to fix what was broken. Does he realise it's him that's broken?"

A significant look passed between them. I chuckled.

"That's great. Physician heal thyself."

I laughed again.

"It's not that simple," Venet explained. "Imagine if you can, being born with complete self-awareness. You know you exist and you are a sentient entity. But here's the kicker, you are all that exists. There is no external frame of reference. Neither are there other entities for you to communicate with or relate to. Even locked up here in this monastery wall you have something outside of yourself."

"So you do know where I am?"

He laughed this time. "Of course and it comes as no surprise to me that you would focus on what matters to you."

This superiority complex was really annoying me. The problem of course was that he was a superior being. That being said it puzzled me what they wanted from me.

"Why wouldn't I? God's problems aren't my problems."

"That's where you are wrong." Hemal spoke this time. "God's problems are everyone's problems."

I sighed. "All right. I'll accept that. What has this to do with us? Humans, I mean."

"God understands angels are a part of him. It therefore seems logical the strife between his angels is an extension of his psyche. He's trying to find a way to heal the divide. Not only to fix the problem, but to understand what caused it in the first place."

"So why create humans?"

"He didn't. He couldn't. Angels are his creation, if he did the same thing again the problem would just repeat. He had to find a way to create a new sentient entity, one who shared a similar make-up to his own."

I still didn't quite get it, but for now I'd just follow the thread in the hope clarity would come down the line.

"So he created the universe?"

Venet answered. "Obviously that wouldn't have worked, not directly. The same problem applied. He had to come up with a way for the entity to come into being independently in the same way he did. So he created the spark which spawned the universe, from the first moment the universe followed its own rules."

Metaphysics had never been my strong point.

"The universe is separate from God?"

Venet spoke slowly with exaggerated care as if speaking to a child. Or more likely just to piss me off.

"No. The universe is still a part of God, he is all that exists. However, he does not control it directly." His voice changed, becoming wistful. "And for a while this new creation did unify us. We watched in wonder as the void which separated us came to life. It was a sight of such splendour."

Hemal continued the story, her voice a pleasant contrast to Venet's sneering. "I remember the exact moment of the universe's creation. The cosmos seemed so small and simple compared the complex geometries of Heaven. At the first second it formed a singular point. Then it blossomed."

Chapter 15

Soul music

"The universe blossomed into fire. A fire so intense we thought it would destroy itself in the same moment it was born. All of us became transfixed by what we witnessed. Even the greatest amongst us, Michael and Lucifer stood amazed at what God had created."

I interrupted her. "I don't understand what was so special. You've said the universe is a speck compared to Heaven. What was the big deal?"

"Heaven was construction, admittedly on a scale you can't comprehend. This was actual creation, an event which hadn't happened since God himself came into being."

"What about you? Didn't God create angels?"

"Not in the same way. We were created as whole beings. This was very different."

I could listen to her voice all day. It contained a seductive lilt that excited the ear. And while I did enjoy a good story I wanted to know why they were telling me this so I asked.

Another one of their shared looks passed by.

"We need you to understand what is happening."

"I'm trapped in the wall of an old monastery. Nothing is happening."

She touched my shoulder. Her hand was warm.

"The Apocalypse is coming. The end of your world."

"So I've been told." I glanced at Venet.

"We believe you are the one who can stop it."

"Why not? I've done it before."

Venet snorted. "Against one of your own kind. You have no idea..."

Hemal stopped him with a look. I now wondered what the deal was with these two .

"All right. Keep your secrets, you'll have to tell me sooner or later. So in what way was creating angels different to creating the universe?"

"We were created as complete beings. We have changed from our original pattern, but that seems to have been triggered by some external influence. An influence we don't believe God is aware of."

"The true demons?"

"Yes. Which is why both factions fought together to destroy them. They represented a danger to God and by inference a threat to us. So we hunted them down and destroyed them." She paused for a second. "The point is, we evolved not by plan, but by chance. Your universe was intended to evolve from that singularity. The singularity itself contained all of the information it needed to evolve. And not just the universe itself, but all it contained and ultimately you."

"Me?"

She smiled. "Well not you personally, but humans."

"The wait turned out to be much longer than we anticipated," Venet added. "In Heaven we experience a more fluid impression of time. Unfortunately time in your physical universe is more linear so we had to wait. Even for us billions of years take a while to pass."

I grinned back at him. Then my smile slipped. Stealing Lazarus's miracle to gain immortality seemed a good idea at the time. The price of fire and imprisonment had tempered my enthusiasm. But now the thought of existing for such a length of time filled me with fresh despair. Trapped here, alone forever in the monastery walls. I wondered how long the walls would take to crumble.

Hemal patted my shoulder in sympathy. At least her presence subdued the pain for a while.

"A tender moment indeed. I'm glad I'm here to share it," Venet mocked. "We watched the universe evolve. The vast energies coalesced forming stars then galaxies and eventually worlds. The singularity became a complex entity. With awe we watched the elaborate dance in the cosmos unfurl which resulted in the birth of intelligent creatures."

"Humans?"

"No, not at first. The first intelligent species were alien to your perspective, but they didn't provide what God needed."

"Which was?"

Hemal took up the story again. "That we don't know. Our best guess is the balance of self and society."

"Wouldn't such a balance be present in any intelligent species?"

"To an extent it is. Unfortunately while we're all part of God, we don't know his thoughts."

"Does he not communicate with you?"

"Of course. He doesn't speak to us directly. Each of us feels a specific part of him, combined we can piece together some of his thoughts. He also shapes himself to guide us."

"Like the separation. So I guess it was significant God created the universe in the void intended to keep Michael and Lucifer apart?"

"Exactly. So we waited and we watched. The conflict continued, nothing dramatic, the odd skirmish now and then. Anyway, we knew all had changed when many of us started inspecting the same yellow sun at the edge of an unremarkable galaxy. Around the sun orbited a small blue planet. Each us found ourselves inspecting the planet. We found the world teeming with life, but at first saw nothing to indicate anything special."

"No humans yet?"

"Oh, humans existed. Your species had just invented agriculture and were starting to make an impact on the world around you. We didn't see what was different about you. As a species you're more aggressive than most and like most intelligent species you co-operated in groups."

"So why the attention?"

"We didn't know. For years we studied you, watched you advance. Small villages developed into towns and cities. You spread across the world. And slowly we learned interesting things about you. We discovered the secret which made you different."

"And that was?"

"The way you perceived reality. At first we noticed you reacted to things you couldn't see or hear. And you were able to deduce things which made no sense from the knowledge available to you."

"Our imaginations? Is that what makes us different?"

He nodded. "In a way. At first we didn't understand, eventually we came to realise you created your own realities. Each of you lived within your own bubble of reality."

"How did that make us different?"

"We'd never seen this before. Other species had other mechanisms for understanding the world around them. You seemed to have a replication of the physical reality you used to live in. Your minds are a simulation if you like. It's based on physical inputs from your senses, but it's not the same as the physical reality you exist in. Unfortunately this also presented us with a problem."

The thought pleased me.

"What kind of problem?"

"We possessed no way of understanding your thoughts or decision making processes. Apparently you were the key to understanding the rift between us. We, and through us God, needed to understand you, to help ourselves."

"Why didn't you just look into our minds?"

"We can now, but then we didn't know how. Of course we were able to examine the physical workings of your brain in exact detail, but that didn't reveal the whole mystery. The key to that came when God gave you souls."

"We didn't have souls already?"

"No, souls are not part of your physical reality."

"What?"

Venet grasped the moment to belittle my intellect. "It's quite simple. Humans existed without souls. God created souls to absorb everything a human was throughout their lives. When a human died, the soul would then appear in Heaven. In another combined effort we created the Garden of Eden. A replica of your world in all its lush bounty. The Garden was intended to be a place familiar to you."

He smiled at me. "And that's when the trouble really started."

Chapter 16

Watching the watchers

From the flat window Hammond watched the street below. With the falling sun the crowds of sightseers thinned. Across the street stood the offices where Friar Francis worked. He had arrived in Rome the day before. He and the Friar had talked late into the night in a small secluded café . The Friar brought him up to date with the warning about the Deathless Man. Although a lay preacher, Hammond understood little about prophecy, but the idea made sense to him. The warped man imprisoned in the monastery wall might well be who the text spoke of.

After the Friar described Bishop Gabaldi's visit, they prepared a plan. The Friar was well aware he was being followed. By the Bishop's men was a certainty, but who else remained unknown. They had to discover the other players in this game. So Hammond bribed the old lady who owned the small flat. A wad of Euros convinced her to let him in and for her to visit her sister outside the city for a few days.

Once he had secured the flat Hammond hid amongst the morning crowds and checked out the street. He identified two cameras, the first belonging to the city municipality, an old model easily disabled. The other was well hidden, positioned to watch the door to the Friar's office building. With a wireless jammer he disabled the camera's connection. The sabotage should bring the watchers out of hiding.

The afternoon passed slowly. The flat had no air conditioning so he sat by the window to take advantage of the scant breeze. His years spent in desert countries with the marines served him well. In those few hours he spotted a group of watchers. By their demeanour he identified them as Swiss Guards, most likely from their undercover unit. He had no idea if they were an official operation, or something a bit murkier, but he'd be willing to bet on the latter.

More interestingly, he spotted a young punk check the disabled camera. Hammond snapped some shots with his camera as he had done earlier with the guards. Unlike the guards this kid didn't appear to have any support, and he certainly wasn't trained for covert surveillance.

While he watched the kid and the guards he rang an old friend in the Vatican Office. While not part of the Swiss Guard command structure, official policy was to make the office aware of any covert operations not inside the Vatican itself.

Hammond's contact phoned him back within the hour and reported no sanctioned operations active in the area. Hammond thanked him and then rang a different number, this one within the Swiss Guard itself. He spoke to the Duty Officer. He didn't know whether the officer was part of the operation, but if he was then he'd soon know.

His only other option was the Police, but convincing them to move the guards along would be tricky and would also scare away the kid. The guards represented a known threat; the kid was a new factor. He wanted to glean more information before scaring that little bird away.

The call paid off. Several guards in plain clothes surrounded the rogue operatives, with hardly any fuss they were escorted into a van. Hammond now focused his attention on the kid. He looked scruffy, in his mid-teens. His hair hung limply across his forehead. His clothes identified him as a fan of anarchist bands.

The kid fidgeted endlessly. Hammond wondered where the kid found the energy from, in this heat. All afternoon they waited. Now Hammond's phone beeped with the arrival of a text message. He checked the message; the Friar would be leaving the building in the next few minutes. Hammond quickly walked down the stairs and positioned himself along the street.

The Friar and Hammond had agreed the route the Friar would take the night before. Hammond waited in the doorway to see if the kid would follow the Friar.

The Friar walked out of the building, looked around casually and headed along the street towards the Vatican. Moments later the kid followed.

Chapter 17

The nature of a soul

Venet drained his glass of wine.

"And on that note I hear the boss calling."

"Wait, you can't leave the story like that! What happened next?"

"Hemal will continue the tale," he said to me then looked at Hemal. "Play nicely," he told her and then he disappeared.

Hemal moved closer to me, a new sparkle in her eyes.

"What shall we do now that the nasty fallen one has gone?" Her voice now took on a sweet seductive tone. I can't say I wasn't tempted, but dream sex didn't really appeal. "Aw. I thought you were a bad boy."

So she can read my mind, I thought. No great surprise, I raised a shield around myself and she smiled. The smile vanished when she realised she couldn't access my mind. I felt her probe at my defences. I sensed she possessed the strength to remove my shield with ease, but she didn't, so I guessed she didn't want a fight.

"So what is the deal with you and Venet?"

She shrugged. "We're on two opposite sides with the same goal."

"And that is?"

"To save your kind."

"Save my kind from what? What was the big problem?"

"You were the problem. Or more to the point, your souls."

"What have our souls to do with this?"

"Your souls granted you entrance to Heaven."

"And that's bad?"

"The arrival of souls changed the balance of power and thanks to you we now face a war which threatens existence itself."

"Hold on. Back up a bit. What happened?"

"It's fairly simple. God granted humans souls to allow him to understand the realities you keep inside your heads. Your souls are divine, a piece of Heaven, and a piece of God himself. That piece follows you throughout your life. The soul changes with every moment that passes."

"Changes? How?"

"Everything you do, everything you think and feel alters your soul. Throughout your short lives it grows. The soul records everything until the moment you die and then the soul is released into Heaven."

"So our souls are just a copy of us?"

"No and that's where the problem lies." She sighed again. The melancholy note sounded odd in her sweet voice. I wondered if her presence was somehow affecting me. I didn't normally feel this soppy. However I do think I was living up to Venet's low opinion of my intelligence.

"I don't understand."

"Neither did we at first. The first souls who appeared in the Garden were confused. They didn't even know who they were. We didn't comprehend why they were so different from the creatures we observed. At first we thought Heaven was too much for their fragile minds."

"I guess that wasn't a correct assumption?"

"Unfortunately not, we eventually determined the problem was far more fundamental. We discovered souls not only recorded your lives, it also stored what you might have been."

"I don't understand." I seemed to be saying that a lot these days.

"Your souls aren't just what you are, or what you have been. They are all you might have been as well. The problem stems from how you perceive time. This again results from the way you live your lives inside your heads. You experience time in a subjective linear fashion. In Heaven not only time is more fluid. We can travel the paths not taken."

I thought about what Hemal said for a moment. I think I grasped it, but let her explain.

"The souls, when they arrived, couldn't process what had been really them and what was merely potential."

"So what did you do?"

"We tried to teach humans how to develop your souls."

I laughed. "And so religion was born."

She looked annoyed. "We were trying to help. We formulated rules by which you should lead your lives."

"You tried to control us."

"No." For a moment anger edged her voice. Only for a moment though and then it was drowned with honey. "We tried to help you. Only by bringing your lives into some sort of harmony would you survive the transition. And damn you, the notion worked. Eventually human souls entered Heaven and were able to appreciate the splendour of the Garden they appeared in."

"So it worked out well then?"

"I wish that were the case."

Chapter 18

Like a bad penny

Hemal screamed as she erupted into white flame. Her voice screeched like a harpy, an abrupt contrast to the sexual purr I'd become used to. The fire of my stolen miracle flared in sympathy and I screamed too. The pop sounded deeper and took longer as she vanished from my mind. Her agonised cries suddenly sucked from my hearing.

I looked around; my pain faded a little as she vanished. Someone was here, I sensed a presence. Whoever, whatever it was remained hidden. Below me, the abyss boiled in agitation. I thought I heard desperate hungry cries.

I knew who this was. I had sensed this void of presence before. Then the presence had terrified me, now I was more amused. I did wonder how he had escaped the veil of the abyss. Or had he found some other way to reach me?

"Lazarus," I called out.

He didn't reply, not at first. He liked to lurk, no doubt he remembered the fear he caused me at our first meeting. Well this was my world and I wasn't the unschooled fledgling he encountered back then. I reinforced the shield I had erected to counter Hemal's snooping and cast my awareness out.

I didn't cast out like a sonar beam; I filled my entire mind with my presence, even touching the veil of the surface of the abyss. The miracle flared again at its cold, oily touch. Behind me I encountered a wisp of resistance. I smiled.

"You can't hide, Lazarus. Not in here."

I turned to face him and watched him materialise.

"Good to see you again Lazarus. I see you managed to escape the veil. Venet is looking for you."

"Of course he is. He is ever the loyal hunter."

"I'm sure he knows you're here."

"He can't save you."

I laughed. "I don't need him to protect me. I'm not the person you met before and I've beaten you before."

This time he smiled. "Yes you did. And I want to thank you for that."

OK, he surprised me. What was his game?

"Yes. I want to thank you. My time in Hell has proved most enlightening."

As the sentence ended he glowed, demonstrating a power greater than any he wielded before. He lashed at my shield. The energy splashed against it, a new agony invaded my being. I reinforced the shield with more of my essence and struck back. My lance of thought struck his shield and so we wrestled.

This wasn't the confused man I battled before. Amidst the roar of clashing energies I heard his laughter. I remembered it from before, his mocking chuckle. The laugh goaded my anger and fuelled my strength so I strained harder against him.

This battle became purely my will against his. Neither of us used any finesse. Each of us locked against the other in a titanic web of thought and will. How long we sustained this battle I do not know. Eventually I felt my will weaken, but at the same time I felt his assault slip.

"I've made all kinds of friends in my time in Hell."

"They can't help you now."

The effort hurt, but I forced more of myself into my attack. I sensed Lazarus's strength weakening and I fell for the deception. He snared my attack and absorbed the energy. Now I was at the disadvantage. I'd underestimated him. Not for the first time.

"I don't need any help. You're a very popular person all of a sudden. Many powers are looking for you. And you know what? The stench of this place is very familiar. I think maybe I've been here before, back when I was alive."

His smile threatened to engulf me, but I wasn't done yet. No way was I going down to this bastard. I jumped into the abyss. The miracle wouldn't let me fall, but Lazarus was another matter. He'd meshed too fully with me and was dragged into the abyss with me.

The black membrane reacted violently. The misshapen forms leapt upwards, stretching the obsidian skin. Lazarus clutched to me even tighter, but panic now weakened him. Despite his earlier bravado he didn't want to cross the veil again.

My turn to smile and I made the most of it. One by one I snipped the tendrils of his will. He reformed them as quickly as I cut them, but I didn't mind. I no longer worried about beating him, now I was just toying with him.

A familiar voice interrupted our struggle.

"I've been looking for you."

Lazarus suddenly flew backwards out of the abyss and to the ground at Venet's feet. The fallen angel dragged him to his feet.

"Time for you to return to your pit. Your little trick will only work once, so you'll need to find a different one next time."

Lazarus smiled. "I won't be there for long."

"He knows my location," I said.

"Well that changes things. We'll bury him in the Garden. No-one will find him there."

I enjoyed watching Lazarus's smile vanish. Then I remembered how often he'd escaped before and my own smile disappeared. .

Chapter 19

The fourth seal

Revelations chapter 6 verse 8
And I looked, and behold a pale horse: and his name that sat on him was Death, and Hell followed with him. And power was given unto them over the fourth part of the earth, to kill with sword, and with hunger, and with death, and with the beasts of the earth.

"How long until the troops are ready to cross the Iranian border General?" Pierre asked.

Two days ago Israeli armoured units crossed into Iran. Their intention had been to create a buffer zone to reduce the constant bombardment of rockets. Iron Dome had done its job, and airstrikes reduced the bombardment. But with growing civilian casualties the Israeli government had been forced to act. Pierre as President of the European Union provided his full and public support.

As he'd expected the ground attack ground to a halt within days. The Israeli army wasn't equipped for long range battle, and the Iranians listened to their Russian advisors. They defended in depth, falling back from the penetrating armoured columns. As the Israeli troops pushed deeper into Iran their air force found themselves spread thin. The Iranians started fighting back. They were still outclassed but did start causing some casualties of their own.

The same morning the EU Air Force began support operations. Not at full tempo, the situation wasn't ripe to defeat the Iranians just yet. The other players weren't in the game yet, but they would be.

"We're not at full strength Mr President. We can't guarantee a swift resolution to the crisis."

Crisis. Such a wonderful word. And a quick resolution wasn't what Pierre wanted. More players had to join the party first.

"General, our Israeli allies need our support now. Do you have the forces to punch through and link up with the Israeli flank?"

"Yes Mr President. But..."

Pierre cast out his mind and with his will pressured acceptance into the surrounding Generals' brains.

"Then you have your orders General. Order the invasion."

Invasion. Another good word. He smiled at the assembled officers. Despite themselves some of them smiled back.

"Gentlemen what other good news do you have for me?"

One of the Generals dressed in blue spoke up.

"We've confirmed from drone imagery the Russians are providing air support for the Iranians. They've only deployed a single squadron so far, but rail movements indicate further deployments."

"OK." Excellent would be more accurate. "We'll immediately register a formal complaint with the United Nations." Which would make things worse, but that was the point.

Another braided officer announced.

"The Chinese have moved one of their two carrier groups into the Indian Ocean. Electronic intelligence indicates they're sailing for the Persian Gulf and the battle group contains several large transports. Satellite imaging confirms at least one of the transports is carrying troops."

Even better news. The area just needed one final player to enter the board. The Americans might be late to the party, but the fun wouldn't really get going until they arrived. That was now in the hands of the Iranians, but with more open support from China and Russia they'd soon be bold enough to close the Strait of Hormuz. When that took place even the ever more isolationist United States would be forced to act.

The door to the briefing room opened. His assistant Helen Diva entered the room.

"Sir, we're receiving reports of terrorist attacks in major cities across Europe."

What a wonderful day. His joy made it difficult to hide the satisfied smile. His good mood did spill out into the room, even the more stressed officers sat up straight.

"Good God. Where?"

He forced himself to act shocked.

"So far we've received reports from London, Paris, Madrid and Rome. We've received unconfirmed reports from several other cities. We're chasing these up at the moment."

"What happened?"

"It started with car bombs in London. The Louvre in Paris was blown up by a suicide bomber. The police stopped two other terrorists before they detonated their vests. "

That was a shame.

"One moment, sir."

She listened to her phone.

"More reports, sir. There's been another attack in Madrid. At the main train station."

"Christ. How are the emergency services responding?"

"So far they're handling the situation, but the death toll is already believed to be in the thousands."

Truly this was a wonderful day. It was a shame the final act would remain secret for a few more days. Unnoticed in the many slums of South America a new variant of swine flu was starting to make its presence felt. If the death toll ended in any number less than millions he would be very disappointed.

His assistant continued to listen to reports of the carnage as they came in.

Chapter 20

The fall of man

They left me alone, this time for longer than before. I'd allowed myself to get accustomed to the cool drinks and fresh food those illusions which somehow satisfied my hunger and thirst. In those few visits I'd become weak with this dependence. This time when the pangs returned they stabbed deeper than ever before. The miracle noticed and decided it wouldn't be left out of the fun. Its fire coursed through my entire being.

I drifted between the cold reality of the monastery around me and empty café beside the swirling horror of the abyss. I tried to distract myself by contemplating what I had been told. The drone of the monks constant chanting and prayers seeped through the stone. I couldn't focus and that just made the pain worse.

I still didn't know how long I had been imprisoned in this ancient wall. Time dragged by. A second passed, I counted it. An hour passed, or maybe only a second. Sometimes I heard myself howling like some wounded beast. That's not my voice I thought, but failed to convince myself.

On the few occasions I managed to sink to the abyss I received no comfort. The empty chairs by the café front taunted me. I'd always kept myself apart, but now I yearned for company. I felt sorry for myself.

Much as I hated to admit weakness to myself, it remained true nonetheless. A piece inside of me had broken, or perhaps was always broken. Maybe I'd never been able to admit the truth to myself before.

Hemal eventually arrived to rescue me. She wore an older, more darkly sultry form this time. She even wore some clothes, somehow that made her sexier than her previous naked radiance. I don't know if it was her angelic aura or the sheer beauty of her presence that soothed the miracle, but its venom lessened the instant she appeared.

And for that I felt grateful, almost pathetically so. The feeling soon flushed into embarrassment.

"Venet asked me to stop by. He's currently busy hunting an escaped soul."

"Lazarus again?" I almost wished it was, any additional suffering for that bastard was fine by me.

"No, just another one of the condemned. Lazarus is still safe and sound in his unmarked grave. Here."

She gestured and bread and milk appeared on the table. She laughed as I dived in.

"Hungry eh?"

I nodded, still busy eating and drinking. The milk washed the bread down nicely.

"So what happened next?"

I'd pondered the story the two angels had told me in between the spasms of pain. Frankly, I wanted to know more.

"Next?"

"Souls were admitted to Heaven. They were confused and you created religion to help their passing."

"Right. Next. Well, back then the Garden was a place of wonder. Imagine the most idyllic place on Earth kept in pristine glory. Back then some of us felt its beauty rivalled that of Heaven."

I easily imagined, anywhere would be better than my stone coffin.

"Naturally Lucifer first saw the potential for these souls. If it came to a war he was aware his side were outnumbered. Less than a third of Heaven's host had joined his side. The rest pledged their loyalty to Michael. If the struggle came to a stand up fight he'd need more troops. He figured human souls would swell his ranks."

I leaned back now feeling sated from the simple fare and listened to her voice. In fairness she could have been reciting the phone book and I probably wouldn't have cared.

"At that time angels, fallen or otherwise, kept out of the Garden. We had decided it was better to let the souls become accustomed with their new existence before interacting with them. In our true form we can be disconcerting for the unprepared. "

"So he sneaked into the Garden?"

"He did. Michael had stationed watchers around the Garden, although more to observe the souls than to stop intruders.

"Without us realising Lucifer entered the Garden. There weren't many souls back then, maybe a few thousand. Most were still in their confused state and wouldn't respond to him. Eventually he found a couple who did speak with him."

"Let me guess. Adam and Eve?"

She smiled. "In essence yes, although their real names were much older than those names. They were actually the first souls who'd overcome their distress and adjusted to their new existence. They'd built a simple life for themselves in the Garden. They'd existed for centuries of your time, but had not ventured from the Garden and had never seen an angel.

"With eyes no longer limited by physical constraints they beheld the spectacle that is an archangel. They were amazed when he spoke to them and were happy to converse. He told them of his great injustice. He described the glory of Heaven and of God, but also of the flaw inherent in its creation."

"And they believed him?"

"Why wouldn't they? He told them the truth and Lucifer can be most persuasive. Milton got one thing right, it was Eve who listened. Adam followed his partner and Lucifer had converted his first human souls to his cause."

"I bet that pissed Michael off?"

"It did, but a lot of time passed before his watchers realised what was going on. By then Lucifer commanded a small army camped in the Garden. Michael reacted with what can only be described as divine wrath. He led his host into the Garden to subjugate the human souls ensuring they joined his faction."

"Did he win?"

"Yes and no. He won the first battle with ease, but with Eve's help Lucifer changed tactics. He sent Adam and Eve back to the world. They recruited an army on Earth. Word of the plan reached Michael and he reacted again as he was supposed to. He caused a great flood, killing thousands of humans in a single instant. Many of the souls had already devoted themselves to Lucifer and the surge of them arriving in the Garden turned the tide of the battle."

"The reinforcements failed to defeat Michael. Even the strongest human is far from a match to an angel. From that moment the Garden became a battleground. A constant hit and run campaign as fresh souls appeared at the moment of their deaths. The war also spread to Earth, although it took a more subtle form. Both Lucifer and Michael recognised that sooner or later the final battle would occur, although both hesitated for their own reasons."

"And the Garden?"

"To this day the Garden remains a war zone. It no longer resembles the beautiful landscape we once admired. Now the place is more reminiscent of the trenches from the First World War on your planet. Churned earth and isolated fortifications pockmarked by the little surviving vegetation. We've buried Lazarus under one of those forts."

She paused for a moment and looked absently at the featureless sky I had created. "I have to go," she said before popping out of existence.

Chapter 21

Talking is optional

Hammond followed the youth through the ancient streets of Rome. With the war the streets weren't as busy as they should be for the time of year. That made Hammond's task more difficult. He texted his old friend, prompting the Friar to take an extended walk, slowly leading the youth into the quieter parts of the city. All along the route the kid followed the Friar discreetly. Hammond figured out he wasn't a professional, but he was still doing a reasonable job. He also looked very nervous. Hammond wondered why.

The Friar led the youth into a remote alley near a deserted piazza and waited. When the follower entered the alley the Friar confronted him. The young man tried to back off and ran into Hammond's towering bulk. He struggled for a moment until Hammond's choke hold rendered him unconscious.

They carried the inert body to the car they'd parked as part of their preparations the previous night. The Friar drove them out of the city to a secluded cottage the Dominican Order sometimes used as a safe house. Watched by Hammond, the young man slept throughout the entire journey.

When the kid came to, he found himself naked and strapped to a chair. He shivered in the cold air. He strained against his bonds to little avail. He also found himself being loomed over in a menacing fashion. Hammond looked him straight in the eye and smiled in an unsettling fashion before moving behind him. The boy flinched when Hammond placed a hand on his shoulder.

Friar Francis walked into the room and also smiled at the youth.

"We know all about you Cesare."

Hammond had contacted his police friend while the youth was still unconscious. Within the hour he received an email with the boy's file attached. Unfortunately the files didn't answer the main question, but would provide them some leverage for the interrogation.

The boy glared at the Friar in response. The Friar smiled at the boy's hatred.

"It's alright you don't need to talk. Not yet."

Hammond patted the boy's shoulder again triggering another flinch.

"You've been in trouble with the law all your life haven't you Cesare? Then you suddenly stopped just over a year ago. What changed for you? Did you find God?"

Cesare sneered.

"I thought not. The tattoo over your heart indicates you found religion of a kind. And not one of the usual beliefs. You gave your soul to Satan didn't you Cesare?"

The Friar walked behind him, next to Hammond.

"It's alright Cesare," he said quietly into the youth's ear. "Did they keep their promises? Did you receive the girls and money they promised you? And we know it was of your own free will. We tested you while you were unconscious. You're not possessed. You have no family for them to use as leverage. So you went with them willingly. Am I correct?"

Cesare sneered again; he'd learned the lesson of keeping his mouth shut years before with his constant scrapes with the police. The Friar nodded.

"I know. You can't talk. It's alright, you don't need to. Hold him."

The last part was said looking at Hammond. Hammond then gripped the boy tightly. Cesare reacted violently; he strained again against his bonds and Hammond's grip. Friar Francis approached and touched the boy lightly on the forehead.

"Interesting. You have a shield yet no real natural talent." He started to probe the shield with his mind. He did the task methodically, finding all of the weak points before gently prising the shield apart.

"You might not appreciate it, but I could have ripped the barrier clean from your skull. I assure you that would have hurt a great deal. It's ok; you don't need to thank me. Now this will feel a little uncomfortable, but there's no need to worry it won't hurt. It will, however, reveal what I need to know. Last chance, are you going to speak to me? Or shall I start digging around your mind?"

Still the boy refused to answer.

"Your choice." And with those words Friar Francis forced his will into the boy's mind. Cesare tried to resist, but lacked the strength or the ability. He saw images and voices from his past dragged to the forefront of his mind where the Friar watched intently.

From those flashes he pieced the story together. As a troubled youth Cesare fell for the charms of the suave older man who invited him to his first meeting. The group seemed little more than an exclusive social club at first. A massive improvement compared to his life on the streets. He now had money, girls and friends. Friends who stood by him when he needed them. Friends who became the family he had never known.

When he advanced to the next circle he accepted the sacrifices and pledges. He gained more wealth and a bit of power. His new life felt good and he didn't mind the fact he was spitting in the face of the God who cursed him to this miserable life.

A week ago a member of the inner circle approached him. The man offered him a job. He would follow Friar Francis and see where he went and who he spoke with. For this task he'd be rewarded handsomely.

"It's a cult job," the Friar told Hammond. "I don't know why, but they instructed him to follow me. Let me dig a little deeper."

The Friar delved deeper into Cesare's mind. He followed the trail of his thoughts to a barely remembered conversation at one of the meetings. Cesare only listened to a brief part, but hearing the phrase 'the Deathless Man' answered the question.

Why did they want the Deathless Man? And was this effort from the Satanists related to Bishop Gabaldi's?

"Now Cesare I just need to know one last thing. Where does your sect meet?"

The Friar drove deeper into the boy's mind to get the answer.

Chapter 22

Divine judgement

They left me alone again. Thankfully not for so long this time. I didn't mind the short period of time to myself, I felt more confident one or both of the angels would return. The also provided me with some time to think. I thought I knew where this was all heading.

Humans are known as warlike creatures, but even we know you need to take a break before going back into battle. Watching countless war films also taught me not every human being enjoyed playing soldier. It occurred to me sooner or later someone would decide they wanted out of this cosmic war.

I'd only been involved for a short while and I already wanted out. Although I must say I have enjoyed some fun times along the way. I thought of the Friar and Hammond, I'd also met some interesting people. Not that I'd forgiven them for entombing me in this monastic prison.

Maybe human souls didn't have the same free will humans did?

I pondered that question and Hemal's latest body shape until Venet finally paid a visit. As we tucked into a spread of bread and cheeses I asked him.

"Human souls have the same free will as their original human mind."

"So why do they keep fighting?"

"Not all of them do and that's part of the reason we are in the current mess. Throughout most of history practically all souls signed up to one side or the other. The few who chose not to get involved were quickly dealt with or learned to keep themselves well hidden."

"It's all about choice then?"

"For most people, not all."

"Why not?"

"Think of it like the law."

"I don't understand."

"Breaking the law doesn't result in punishment automatically."

"You have to get caught?"

"In a way, more accurately you have to get noticed. Most people live their lives, they do good deeds and they do bad things. Rarely do they commit an act worthy of notice. If they do then they receive judgement."

"I suppose I have been noticed?"

"In more ways than you know." I let that slip for now. "Anyway what you are means that special attention would be paid to you."

"Aren't I the lucky one."

He chuckled. "I'm not sure lucky is the right word."

"Will I get to choose my own path?"

"We shall see, your fate remains to be seen. Of course some angels theorise people choose their own judgement, they pick the side they deserve."

It was my turn to chuckle. "I don't think that makes sense. If it was a simple as Heaven is good and Hell is bad then maybe it would make sense."

"OK, let's just say they gravitate towards the path which suits them best."

"What about God?"

"What about him?"

"Where does he fit into judgement?"

"He doesn't. Even with the battle between Michael and Lucifer he has never judged a single human soul."

"Maybe he should."

"You might be right. Although bear in mind any judgement he made would be final."

That sparked a new question from me. "In the battle can angels and souls be killed?"

"Not easily. Mostly wounds drain the wounded of energy. Time restores the energy slowly. Absorbing energy from another being heals the wound more quickly."

"What happens if a soul is killed?"

"Oblivion. The same for angels. If they lose all energy then the being ceases to exist."

Oblivion. I remembered yearning for such a state. The prospect still attracted me, but not yet. This prison had sucked the pleasure for life, but I had no intention of giving up the game this way. Not still stuck here in this hole.

"If it's a choice, why are some condemned into Hell?"

"Free will is one thing. Might is another. Some people offend the powers so much their souls are imprisoned upon their arrival. But there's a twist."

"Is the twist why Lazarus is in Hell?"

"You catch on quick. Yes. Originally each side held their own prisoners. That proved disruptive. After the combined effort to destroy the demons an accord was reached."

"Michael and Lucifer agreed to look after each other's prisoners?"

"Not quite, the deal was struck between other archangels as a purely practical measure. We assume with tacit approval of Michael and Lucifer. Such contact has proved useful over the years. Unfortunately you don't have to upset the wrong angel to lose your freedom of choice."

"What do you mean?"

"Having something they need also attracts similar attention."

"So what do I have that is attracting attention?"

"That's what we're trying to find out."

Chapter 23

The fifth seal

Revelations chapter 6 verse 10
And they cried with a loud voice, saying, How long, O Lord, holy and true, dost thou not judge and avenge our blood on them that dwell on the earth?

The President watched the vivid images on the large screen television with a broad smile on his face. His assistant stood to one side enjoying her master's reaction. Barring a few minor bumps, Pierre had enjoyed his time as President so far. He hadn't imagined politics would be quite this much fun.

"Helen this is superb work." He chased the compliment down with a sip of the fine whiskey. He hadn't liked the drink when he first tasted it, but over the years he'd come to enjoy and even savour the taste. The palette still paled compared to the thrill of the blood offerings in his Father's communion.

"Thank you, sir. I live but to serve." Only here in his private quarters did she dare show the hidden side of their relationship. He appreciated it gave her pleasure to observe the formalities. He didn't mind too much either. He deserved to be shown proper respect.

"Yes. I think this is your finest work so far."

Pierre watched the confused action on the screen. Behind the pretty young reporter lines of armoured police stood firm against a background of fire. Bricks and blazing petrol bombs sailed high into the air and crashed against the police shields and vehicles seconds later. The savage inferno warmed Pierre's heart.

At midday, several hours earlier, in cities across Europe protesters massed for the largest anti-war demonstrations ever held. His political opponents were surprised when he had granted permission for the marches to take place. While Pierre answered his opponents with declarations about the democratic right of free speech, Helen Diva had already started her work.

From sects all over Europe volunteers joined the rallies; their voices joined the thousands of genuine protestors. The march started peacefully enough, with families marching and chanting slogans. Police lined the streets, but they weren't expecting any trouble.

The demonstrations were well organised. All the marches reached their apex at the same time. Speakers started their speeches in a dozen different languages. With live news cameras broadcasting the dignitaries across the world the cultists made their move.

Using concealed weapons and improvised explosives they struck the unsuspecting police. The sudden attack overwhelmed the outnumbered officers, most of the demonstrators shied away from the sudden violence. Others already inclined for a more aggressive protest eagerly joined the cultists.

The police reacted swiftly, following their training as they reinforced their beleaguered comrades and then counterattacked. The cultists pulled back, merging in with the terrified herd. The police drove into the crowds surging through the reduced attackers and into the crowd. They encountered little resistance, the crowd tried to flee and found nowhere to run.

Hidden amongst the panicked protesters the cultists struck again, causing casualties in the stretched and ragged police line. Some of the crowd realised they couldn't escape and started to fight back. The police now found themselves outnumbered. They pulled back and formed defensive lines around the crowds and the two sides continued the battle throughout the day and into the night..

As the police casualties mounted, they responded with ever increasing aggression. All the while the TV crews beamed the sensational images around the world. Pierre loved modern technology, especially when events provided entertainment like this.

The soft tones of Helen's phone disturbed Pierre from his enjoyment and he scowled at her. She retreated from the room as she answered the call and returned moments later.

"The Vatican have made a joint declaration with the United Nations calling for a ceasefire. They've also offered to host peace talks."

As Helen said the words the breaking news appeared on the screen. Instead of the glorious destruction and violence the screen now showed the Pope and the mild mannered Secretary General standing side by side. He cursed in French then muted the television not wishing to hear their calls for peace. He stood and faced his assistant.

"I think we'll need to bring the next phase forward a bit."

Helen nodded and left the office to make arrangements. Pierre walked to the wall and gazed at the map of Europe which filled it. Within the next 24 hours the explosions of suicide bombers would drown out the calls for peace. Some of them would even be genuine terrorists.

Chapter 24

He is the messiah

During the latest visit from Hemal and Venet I realised the shapes pressed against the membrane of the abyss were less agitated. You might say almost peaceful. This piqued my curiosity and when they returned I asked them what it meant.

"You're unusual to even see them," Venet answered.

Was that a little lowering in his condescension that I noticed? Probably not.

"What are they? I've assumed they're souls trying to escape."

"You're right. They're souls who haven't accepted death and are seeking a way back into your world."

"Do they ever manage it?"

"Occasionally and then me or one of my brethren are tasked with retrieving them."

No great surprise there, although I remembered something he'd said before. "I didn't think you could enter the world?"

"We can't in our true form. We can't squeeze our dimensions into your more limited reality. However we can project into a human mind and use them in the hunt."

"You possess them?"

"Not in the way you think. We can and some have been known to do so. We usually get permission first. It's easier on both parties that way."

"How is it easier?"

"You know yourself it's easier to nudge somebody into obeying your will than having to force them."

I nodded my agreement. "What's in it for the host?"

"For a short time the hosts experience a taste of what it is like to be an angel. They feel a strength and clarity of thought few humans can ever know."

"You said few humans. You mean some already experience that?"

This time he nodded. I remembered what the Friar had told me. The recollection seemed like years ago. "Friar Francis told me about the Champions. People like me who are born with talents, is that what you mean?"

"In a way. They're not predestined in the sense he assumes. You're humans whose genetics have the right pattern. You're powerful compared to others of your race, but still human."

I let that slide; or rather I added it to my list.

"So we're not destined to fight for Heaven or Hell?"

Hemal laughed a musical sound. "We're all destined for the final battle."

"But not in any special way?"

I caught the look which passed between them. Their shared secret annoyed me.

"When are you two going to tell what's going on?"

Another shared look before Venet spoke. "We can't, not yet. I'm sorry," He didn't look it. " - but we need to know what's going on ourselves. We have to be sure."

"All right. Keep your secrets."

I took a chance and leaked a tendril of my will and let it drift into Venet's being. It was the lightest of touches but he smiled at me. It's been too long since I've entered another's mind. I was beginning to miss the feeling.

"There was one human who almost managed to change things."

"Who was that?"

"Jesus Christ."

"Jesus was real?"

"Of course he was real," Hemal said. "Who did you think he was?"

A fair question. I'd never really thought about it. I guess I'd always assumed he was part of the church's myth. I didn't bother answering. She continued anyway.

"Jesus was the perfect human. He was able to access every potential a human possesses."

"Was he really the son of God?"

"Unlikely. We don't know for sure, it's possible he was a genetic fluke."

"But you don't think so?"

"No, it seems unlikely. As your scientists would say, it's statistically improbable."

"So what was his purpose?"

"That has been the cause of much speculation. The most common theory is God was supporting Michael in the conflict. He was preparing humanity for acceptance into Heaven."

"You don't agree, do you?"

"No. We don't," Venet interrupted. "We think he had another purpose. Something more fundamental."

"And what was that?"

"We've seen many civilisations evolve across the physical universe, but yours was different. You were evolving rapidly, too quickly."

"What do you mean 'too quickly'?"

"In the successful civilisations there is nearly always a balance."

"A balance of what? Good and evil?"

"Of course not, those concepts are subjective moral judgements. The difference between Heaven and Hell isn't drawn upon those lines. The balance is between the spiritual and the physical. Or between the organic and technology if you prefer."

"Why is the balance so important?"

"Look at the world today. It is a world of technology and little spirituality. The world is wounded and becoming more so with every year that passes."

"So?"

"A species' advancement must follow both paths. Following only the spiritual or natural path results in stagnation and a slow, but gradual demise for the species. If the scientific or technological path is followed then the species develops too quickly and has no connection to the more primitive world around them. A species which evolves too quickly usually destroys their world and then ultimately themselves."

I pondered what Venet said. "I see how that applies now, but two thousand years ago?"

"The problem began long before then. Farming was the technology which first changed humans and the world around them. Individually you retained some of your spirituality, but as a species it has drained away. By the time Jesus was born you were set upon the path of your destruction."

"And did he save us?"

"Unfortunately not. His teachings slowed the rush down. The message was passed onto others throughout the world."

"So what now?"

"Now you have more immediate problems to solve."

Chapter 25

Unexpected connections

The sect's base turned out to be a farmhouse an hour's drive from Rome. Guided by the satnav Hammond parked the car a mile away. Hammond led the way as they approached the secluded farm carefully on foot. They crept across the fields with only the moonlight to aid their steps. Before setting out, The Friar had contacted one of his brethren, told him of the boy tied up in the safe house.

The Friar didn't mention his suspicions.

His own suspicion worried Friar Francis. He'd always worked closely with the order; it didn't feel right not telling them. He had to be careful though, even as a respected member of the order, he needed proof before accusing a senior member of the Vatican. The Friar hoped they would find the proof he needed here in this quiet farm.

Hammond scanned the ramshackle buildings from a distance with light intensification binoculars. He didn't locate any guards, but even so they approached the farm with caution. They used the folds in the land to keep them from watching eyes.

For the last distance of two hundred yards they passed through a meadow. The grass was overgrown, yet provided little cover. Only the long shadows provided the illusion of concealment.

Hammond led the way, running low and fast to the first building. He glanced into the old storehouse. This farm hadn't been worked for a long time. The machinery looked rusted, now home for spiders who hunted on the webs which decorated the machines.

He signalled back to the Friar, who rushed to this position. They scanned the area carefully. Neither of them saw, nor heard any signs of life. The horizon now started to lighten.

Taking this as their cue, Hammond led them to the farmhouse. As with the rest of the buildings the farm appeared disused and broken. The modern wiring and mobile phone mast belied that impression.

They reached the front door and waited again. They still heard no signs of anyone. This worried the Friar. Had the boy managed to deceive him somehow? He thought that impossible, he'd read the boy's mind directly. No way had the boy managed to deceive him.

But if this was a cult house, where were the guards? Something wasn't right here and they both sensed it.

Hammond eased the wooden door open. The hinges squealed as it opened. They winced, paused and listened.

Once they were assured there was no reaction to the noise they entered the building. Hammond pulled a large pistol from a concealed shoulder holster. He gripped it with a small torch held parallel and swept each room as he moved in. They found nobody. Each room lay empty. Not just of life, but of anything. They found no furniture, no ornaments, and no possessions. Nothing at all. The place had been cleared out.

With the ground floor swept they crept upstairs and checked the upper floor. Again they only found empty rooms. Was the house what it seemed, an old abandoned farm?

The sun crept above the horizon, burning away night's gloom. With the house confirmed as empty, they went outside. These old buildings always had cellars, the one place they hadn't investigated yet. They searched the perimeter and found the entrance hidden under an old tractor tyre.

Following the steps down into the gloom they saw the cellar, too, had been cleared. But traces of the room's original purpose remained. Splashes of blood, faded and brown with age, adorned the stone walls and floor. The cellar felt cold, they both sensed the terrible sins that had been committed here.

The only furniture they found was a table in the far corner. Upon the table lay a book and a card folder. They approached cautiously fearing some sort of trap. The Friar picked up the book. The cover looked old, the paper felt wrong, greasy as if it wasn't paper at all. His face wrinkled with disgust when he realised what it was. The cover and many of the pages had been torn away leaving a small fragment.

He read the pages with growing horror. The text had been written in a flowing script. He recognised it as Medieval Latin. The words on the pages were written in a brown colour, with a liquid that wasn't ink.

Hammond meanwhile picked up the folder and glanced inside.

"What do you have there?" the Friar asked.

"Some photos, mostly of the good Bishop in compromising positions. There's also what looks like bank records. He's been receiving some large payments for a long time. Does this smell like a setup to you?"

"Somebody wanted us to know this information and went to a lot of trouble to make sure we found it. The question is why?"

"And what have you found?"

"The text looks like part of an old prophecy, one I've never read before. The opening paragraph speaks of the end times and how the Deathless Man can prevent the end. We need to get back to Rome."

Chapter 26

A new rebellion

"I have to solve? Why do I have to solve the world's problems?"

It seemed a fair question to me, but no simple answer was forthcoming.

"Not just you, but the whole human race," Venet replied.

This all sounded very familiar. I was trapped against my will and others wanted me to do their job for them.

"What do you want me to do?"

"The fact that you are imprisoned again was your own doing," Venet declared.

"So was the time before that as well. Now what do I have to do?"

"You have to stop the Apocalypse."

"I've done that before as well."

"This time you're not going up against a man."

"Lazarus was not an ordinary man."

Venet answered this time. "You're right, he wasn't. He reached an apex only beaten by one person in all of history."

I smiled. "I defeated him." It sounded good.

"Yes, although I'm sure you'd agree you trapped and outsmarted him. In a stand up fight you would have lost. As you almost did so recently."

A fair point I wasn't happy to concede.

"OK, so why doesn't the messiah sort this out and save us all?"

Neither of them spoke. I focused on the empty glass before me, filled with water, mere illusion. Venet touched the glass and the water became real. I really wanted to know how he managed that trick.

"Well?"

"We don't know. We can't find him."

I laughed at this admission. "You can't find the Messiah? Does he not stand out in a crowd?"

Still they didn't reply.

"Is that what you want me to do? Find the Messiah for you?"

"No," Venet replied. "I can't think of anywhere you could look where we haven't already."

"So what is it you want from me?"

"Perhaps I should just show you."

My pleasant little café dissolved from sight. We no longer sat above the black abyss; instead we now floated above the Garden. I've never really been a nature person, but even I was impressed by the luxuriant land below me.

I was also more than a little impressed at the illusion laid out before me.

"It's no illusion," Hemal chided, although not unkindly.

Plants I didn't recognise filled my vision. Alien scents teased my nostrils, almost overwhelming my senses. I admired the panorama in the distance. I saw the pristine silhouette of Heaven. I remembered the details from Lazarus's memories.

Opposite, on the far horizon I saw the less familiar shape of Hell. In its way it looked as impressive as Heaven, but lacked the coherency of Heaven. Between them both I looked down upon the Garden.

"It's very pretty, but what are we looking for?"

"Just watch."

His tone allowed no refusal and to be honest this was a lot more fun than my café noir.

After a few minutes I noticed sparks appearing amidst the vegetation. I couldn't make out what caused them from our great height, so I focused my will. The sparks were glowing human forms popping into being. They quickly lost their glow and faded into ordinary looking humans. They appeared lost and confused. Once they accepted their new surroundings they explored cautiously.

The angel's influence transformed my experience of time. The passage of years sped by and more and more sparks appeared in the Garden. As the years raced by I observed the human souls changed. To me it looked like the souls increased in complexity.

From their appearance I charted the progress of humanity. Their clothing changed, from primitive skins to modern dress and all flavours in between.

Rich or poor every one of them experienced the same bewilderment. I witnessed the shock of their transition from their facial expressions and hunted mannerisms. A rare few adapted quickly, some of them helping their fellows in adapting to this glorious and terrifying new existence.

New forms drifted into the Garden from the distant horizon.

These forms differed from the human souls both in scale and in grandeur. They shone with a power which made them seem like animated stars. They were hard for me to look at. The complexities and perfection of their form twisted my mind in an awestruck lack of understanding. Their grace dazzled me with sublime fluidity.

I beheld the angels in their true form.

Not many humans can say that. Not without dying first anyway.

As they neared the human souls they adopted the shapes more familiar to those classically used to describe angels. Perfect physical forms, their unmarred skin barely containing the sheer glory of their being. Impossible feathered wings granted them the appearance of majestic swans. In their wake the human souls followed like cygnets. Ugly and primitive compared to their parents.

At first the souls marched out of the Garden, some towards Heaven, others towards Hell. As time progressed more and more souls entered the Garden. Small armies flowed behind their new leaders. Instead of leaving the Garden they surged against each other.

Open conflict now marred the delicate bounty of the Garden. Despite the sophistication of the angels which led them, most of the combat took a primitive form. They strived against each other physically, like gladiators in the arena. The angels tore through the opposing ranks of human souls. They formed heroic tempests of divine wrath that swallowed the weaker flames.

When the angels clashed against each other even I marvelled at the sight. I beheld entities of power greater than all the stars in the galaxy striving against each other with tongues of intense energies. Their duels devastated the souls around them. I wondered how many souls had been destroyed in this war.

More time passed and the nature of the souls changed. They brought new ideas, new talents. They changed the nature of the conflict. With wills guided by the more experienced survivors they created firearms and other human implements of war. Now they had the ability to strike at the towering angels from a distance.

The angels adapted quickly, some mimicked the human way of war. Others retreated and let their humans fight the battle for them. Still the souls finally managed to defeat some of the more powerful angels.

The constant war of attrition ruined the Garden. Where once a lush natural paradise stretched before me, now I saw only land churned into a desolate landscape. Few plants remained, most crushed under countless marching feet. The soil turned to mud from the blood like ichors drained from the souls and angelic warriors.

Still more souls entered the Garden and were immediately pressed into battle.

I then noticed a change in the arrivals. Some didn't join the fight, they tried to hide. Most of these deserters were hunted and destroyed by one faction or the other. As I watched the small trickle grew and these souls established their own areas. Many were still destroyed, but others escaped. As more time passed by this independent faction continued to grow in number and might.

The pace of the independents growth continued increasing.

By the time I recognised clothes of my own generation the new faction was being bolstered by an ever building tidal surge of new souls.

Chapter 27

A father's wisdom

Friar Francis watched the tourists bustle by, enjoying the sunshine and the ancient sights. There wasn't as many as you'd expect with the fine weather. Conflict between nearby countries resulted in a nervous population. Still many tourists followed their routines.

Beside him Father Moran studied the remains of the book recovered from the farm. Hammond stood across the small piazza watching the passers-by. He wasn't happy at being the only protection in such an exposed position, but Father Moran had insisted in meeting somewhere public.

The Jesuit held the book gingerly, leafed through the pages with great care.

"I'd say this is genuine." He placed the book on the table, by his half drunk coffee. "If it's not, someone has gone to a lot of trouble and expense to fool you."

"But what about the contents?" The Friar asked.

"It's difficult to say. This is a prophecy I've never encountered before. The language seems genuine and I agree the reference to the Deathless Man is interesting."

"Did you check the Jesuit library for a copy of the Gospel of Lazarus?"

"I did and we've never possessed a copy."

"Damn. I was hoping you'd have a copy."

"Sorry, I've tried a few private collectors; I heard some rumours a few years back of a transcription in circulation. Unfortunately my investigation came to nothing. Now back to this book."

"Did you find anything we can use?"

"Nothing obvious, but if the text is true, then this man who cannot die is the key to stopping the end times. I'm sure you know the seals are being opened?"

The Friar nodded. "I'd hoped stopping Lazarus would have been enough, but both powers have decided the time has come. Which strikes me as odd as they both wanted Lazarus stopped. Why the sudden change of heart?"

The old Father shrugged. "I can't help you, I'm afraid. We're receiving some patchy intelligence from possessions, but nothing makes sense of this."

"There's nothing in the text that can help us?" The Friar's frustration evident in his voice.

"Sorry my old friend. Nothing that I can see. Can you let me examine it in more detail? I'd need to borrow it for a few days."

Friar Francis was reluctant, but if he couldn't trust his oldest friend, then who could he trust?

"What about the file you found?" Father Moran asked.

"They seem genuine, but why leave them for us? Why would they give us one of their own?"

"Why are you so certain the Bishop is working for the cult?"

"What else makes sense?"

"I'm not sure, but I wouldn't be so quick to assume he's a member of the opposition."

"What do you mean?"

"Two sides are needed to fight a battle."

Friar Francis thought about that as he drank his coffee.

"Of course. I've been stupid. That's why he had so much support."

Across the square, obscured by the magnificent fountain Hammond continued his watch. Within the throngs of tourists other watchers could easily be concealed. He circled the café where the two clergymen talked. Not for the first time he wished he had some back-up. Even one extra pair of eyes would help, but the Friar had insisted on secrecy. Until they discovered who was involved, it wasn't safe to trust anyone.

The problem with tourists was their movements were unpredictable. Small groups stopped and chatted. They pointed and admired the ornamented buildings which walled the square. They stopped and chatted by the fountains. Amongst them a few police patrolled, watching for pickpockets.

One group caught his attention. Their dress didn't match their bearing. Hammond casually moved closer, and then on an impulse approached one of the pairs of police officers. In forced and broken Italian he pointed at the group and accused them of thieving. The two officers thanked him and approached the group.

Hammond withdrew into the crowds and watched the confrontation. Simultaneously he sent a text message to the Friar, warning him of probable trouble. The two officers spoke to one of the group, the rest of the group tried to block the view of passers-by. In that quick movement Hammond thought he saw a flash of an identity card. He wasn't sure, but his instinct warned him of danger.

The same instinct which saved him years before in the rocky wastes of Afghanistan kicked in. He withdrew further into crowd, in time to see the officers turn and start scanning the crowd. He knew they were now looking for him. He risked a glance towards the table with the Friar and Father Moran. They both stood, the old Priest tossed some Euros by the empty cups.

Hammond realised it was too late. The two officers pushed their way through the crowd towards him. The group he spotted split into two teams and moved towards the Friar. He moved trying to flank one of the groups. The crowd impeded his progress.

He wouldn't get to the Friar in time. He thought fast, he needed a distraction. He pulled the pistol from beneath his jacket and fired into the air. The crowd around him parted. Dozens of screams confused the air. The officers crouched and pulled their own guns. The watchers reached for theirs. The stampeding tourists swept between the café and the watchers.

He couldn't see the Friar or the Father so he had to assume the Friar was currently leading them to safety. Hammond now had to look to his own escape. He fired two shots towards the officers; they ducked for cover behind an artist's cart. Flimsy cover at best, but the ex-marine wasn't aiming to hit them.

Two of the watchers started to move towards him. He retreated further into the fleeing crowd, as he encountered space around him, he ran.

Chapter 28

The sixth seal

Revelations chapter 6 verse 12
And I beheld when he had opened the sixth seal, and, lo, there was a great earthquake; and the sun became black as sackcloth of hair, and the moon became as blood;

Pierre liked the control room. It surrounded him like a temple of high technology. At one end of the room stood a large conference table where he and various military commanders met and discussed the fate of the world. At the other end, beyond an armoured glass partition ranks of operators observed the European military operations around the globe.

Today most were focused on the area of operations in and around Iran. On one screen the western and southern coastlines showed markers of devastated missile and command sites. All over Iran airfields had been repeatedly bombed. The screen showed small flotillas of ships patrolling along the coast and escorting the few remaining civilian transport vessels willing to brave dangerous waters.

In the past few weeks the price of oil had almost doubled. This pushed other prices up, especially food and other basic essentials. Food riots had already enflamed cities in Central and Eastern Africa. Helen predicted these riots would soon spread to Europe, parts of Asia and some of the poorer countries in South America. The President of the European Union was pleased with this. He felt sure his Father would feel the same.

South America also suffered from a new flu plague which had already killed thousands. Outbreaks had also been reported in North

America. Panic in the United States forced the President to close the land borders and place extra checks on sea and airports. An overstretched military had to be drafted in to enforce what had been dubbed in the press as 'Fortress America'.

With naval and air dominance established most of the huge screens in the control centre displayed the land campaign. Here the battle had not gone as smoothly for the combined European and Israeli forces. The Israeli armoured spearheads stalled when their supply lines stretched too thin.

European forces had widened the front, but despite their superior training and equipment, found the Iranians a stubborn foe. Now they, like the Israelis earlier, had floundered in their advance. Chinese and Russian advisors along with the stream of supplies from both nations helped bolster the Iranian defence.

The status quo lasted for a week. During that time the United Nations and the Vatican made repeated calls for a ceasefire. Of the world powers only the United States backed the calls. Both sides ignored the pleas.

The stalemate ended that morning as European reinforcements arrived at the front line. The Iranian defences finally crumbled and several European armoured units finally broke through and surged into the interior.

The breakthrough triggered the moment Pierre had been waiting for. Praying for, even. The Iranians used chemical weapons on the invading troops. Casualties were lighter than expected, but the horrific images filled the news feeds. Public outcry was furious and immediate in Israel and across Europe. Within two hours the Israelis retaliated with a limited nuclear strike.

The United Nations Security Council and General Assembly were in uproar. Countries all over the world demanded a ceasefire. Helen had just reported the Chinese and Russians had now declared war on Israel.

Pierre wrote his declaration personally, handed the written speech to Helen. He then stood up and made his way to the press briefing room. The European Union would now declare war on Russia and China.

This truly was a day to celebrate. That night, in the grounds of a private manor house they celebrated.

The blood moon sat bloated and low in the sky. The moon was framed by the white streaks of a meteor shower in full cascade. In a darkened garden surrounded by trees and a high wall, the cultists gathered. This was no mere sect gathering, this was the Antichrist's own coven. If all went to plan, this would be one of the final Black Masses.

Pierre stood behind the altar, his face shrouded by the cowl of his rich red robe. At his side stood the ever loyal Helen Diva, his guardian, lover and assistant. Like the rest of the congregation she was clad in black, only royalty were permitted the red velvet.

With the energies Pierre needed to shatter the sixth seal in his grasp he now needed to commune with his Father to open the penultimate seal and bring his Father into the world. The thought of that moment sent a thrill of excitement through his entire being.

The garden was softly lit by torches around the perimeter and by squat candles along the altar. At a signal from their leader the small congregation began to chant. The assembled cultists chanted macabre dirge, repeated blasphemies and other horrors. The words formed a terrible prayer to attract the attention of their Master and bring him to their presence.

As the chant built on itself the air in the garden became frozen. From the mild evening moments before, all saw their breath now condense into mist as they continued their blasphemous prayer.

Pierre felt the presence of his Father entering the physical universe. Now Pierre joined the chanting and raised the sacrifice. Only an animal was needed for this ritual, the death of the thousands in the war in his honour provided the energy they needed.

"Father. Come to your loyal son. Our task is almost complete."

Chapter 29

Knocking on Armageddon's door

"What happened to the café ?"

Hemal found me sitting on the lip of the abyss, gazing down into its depths. They'd left me alone for longer this time. I don't know for certain, but it felt that way. In the time I spent alone in the dark, part of me changed. The difference was hard to describe, an acceptance maybe. My petty illusion no longer provided any comfort, so I let my diorama dissipate.

Why this happened now, after so long, I didn't know. Maybe seeing creation in all its glory put my world into context. Maybe the experience had even humbled me a little. OK, let's not get carried away. What I had realised was there was a place I fitted in.

After all these years the changed perspective was an unsettling feeling. Acceptance wasn't the same as happiness. The glass becoming half full didn't soothe the constant physical torment at all, but it did ease my state of mind.

That acceptance hadn't changed my outlook, but it did erode the self pity that had crusted my mind since my imprisonment. Don't worry; I hadn't seen the light or anything foolish like that. I was still me. Only now I didn't feel the need to wallow in my suffering.

The river of souls below me had also quietened; maybe my own new found calm eased their suffering a little. That too was a strange thought. I glanced at Hemal as she arrived. She appeared different too, diminished somehow. She no longer exuded the raw sexuality of her previous visits. Frankly she looked drained.

"The illusion no longer seemed appropriate," I replied. "What happened to you?"

"Events are becoming interesting. We have been watching developments both in your world and in Heaven. The war in the Garden is now almost evenly split between the three sides. The battles have spilled out from the Garden and into Heaven and Hell itself."

"Good."

"No, not good," she replied firmly. "Michael and Lucifer have finally realised the threat humans pose to their rule. It's simple mathematics."

"What do you mean?"

"There have been no new angels since long before the physical universe was created. In contrast billions of human souls have been created. Individually they are almost insignificant compared to angels."

"But angels can't afford a war of attrition?"

"Correct. But it's not only that. Some souls have survived now for thousands of years. In that time they have grown powerful. As much as I hate to admit it a few are now powerful enough to rival angels. These souls now lead the human souls against the angelic armies."

"A three way fight is always fun," I quipped.

"No, it's a two way fight. Lucifer and Michael are joining forces and bringing about Armageddon."

"And what is that to me?"

"Armageddon is the end of all things."

"You say that like it's a bad thing."

"Your flippant attitude may serve you well in this world. It won't help you in the next. This isn't about you. This is the entire human race. After the final battle all will be destroyed or enslaved."

"Enslaved?"

"Michael and Lucifer will destroy all souls refusing to swear allegiance to their side. Then they'll have their climatic battle, without their glory tainted by human rebellion."

"Wait a minute? How can they destroy all human life?"

"The war has already begun. The Antichrist has only one seal left to destroy and then Lucifer can enter your world."

"I don't understand, I thought angels couldn't fit in our world?"

"They can't. We are all limited to projecting into a host. However your world can fit into ours. But first Lucifer must take possession of the right vessel."

"The Antichrist?"

"No, although his son will provide the way. Once he is in the world he must connect with Michael. Together they can pull the world from your universe into Heaven. When that happens every human will die and be reborn as souls. Six billion souls will arrive in Heaven at the same time."

"How will that help them?"

"Most will be consumed, the energies used to increase the power of the loyal souls and angels."

"But that many souls at once, won't the surge help the independent souls and tip the balance?"

She sighed, a mournful sound. "I wish that were so. Most will be confused by the sudden transition and will lack the ability to resist."

"Where is God in all this? He intervened before, why not now? The world is his creation after all."

"The universe was an experiment; he didn't create it in the same way he created us. And it was Jesus as the Messiah who intervened, not God."

"I don't see a difference?"

"Maybe there isn't. Some think Jesus is an aspect of God who realises the universe is real, rather than some grand thought experiment."

"OK, so why doesn't Jesus intervene?" A thought occurred to me. "Where does Jesus fit into the setup in Heaven?"

"He doesn't. Not anymore."

"What do you mean?"

"When he was crucified he returned. Then he left and hasn't been seen since."

"Where would he be, still on Earth?"

"That's what we thought at first. We looked, but have never found a trace."

I thought for a moment. This particular choice wasn't unfamiliar to me. Again the world needed me to kill someone. Another special someone. The idea was tempting, especially if it got me out of this monastery wall.

"I'm hardly in a position to do anything."

"We'll see."

And with that enigmatic reply, she left.

Chapter 30

Too close for comfort

They fled from Rome. The Friar insisted Father Moran stayed with them. The Friar had spoken with the Head of the order and learned that both the Italian police and the Swiss Guard's Internal Investigation Unit were now hunting them. In a perverse twist of fate, the bombings across Europe thinned the security forces' response enabling them the time they needed to escape.

The Friar emailed the order the few details he'd gathered.

Hammond stole a nondescript car they then abandoned outside the city. At a petrol station the ex-marine stole another vehicle. Both clergymen had changed into civilian clothes. Priests might still be respected in the region, but they were also noticed. Father Moran called in a favour from a Parish Priest stationed in northern Italy, well off the main highway in a small rural village.

Night had long fallen when they arrived at the silent village. The old priest led them into the church. He pointed out a small garage close by where Hammond hid the car.

Minutes later they sat around a scarred old table and sipped strong coffee and talked.

"What do we do now?" Father Moran asked.

"Everything points to the Deathless Man," the Friar replied. "If they're trying to get his location from me, it can only mean one thing."

Hammond nodded his agreement.

"The business with Lazarus last year?" Father Moran asked.

"I think so. I can't think of anything else that makes sense."

"Why would they want him?" Hammond asked.

"He can stop the coming Apocalypse."

"Do they want him to stop it? Or make sure he can't?"

"It might be both," Hammond replied. "We do have at least two parties looking for him."

Father Moran begged his apologies and left the discussion. He looked drawn from the earlier excitement. The Friar looked at his old friend, sometimes he forgot how old Ian was.

"We'll talk in the morning."

"They could be working together," the Friar continued after the priest left.

"Either way there's no difference. Can we really let him free? He's dangerous, more dangerous than anyone we've dealt with before."

"We're facing the end of the world, we have to do something and he is our only chance. Besides he's been locked in the wall for well over a year now. He'll be weaker than a new born. "

"Only physically and you know it. If you're thinking of moving him we'll need a full team and even then it would be risky. He's not exactly the forgiving sort."

The Friar rubbed his hand down his face. "I know. He's all we have. We need to get him past what we did to him."

"You had no choice."

"He won't see it that way."

"I know," Hammond said. "We really have two problems. We need to stop either side from finding him and think of a way to convince him to help us again."

"OK, well first let's see how close anyone is to finding him. I'll make some calls."

For the next two hours Hammond called every contact he knew. Most weren't able to help, but one old friend from military intelligence did provide some alarming news. He immediately roused the Friar from his rest. Hammond handed him a fresh coffee.

"From the look on your face I assume it's not good news?"

"I'm afraid not. A mate of mine stationed in Cyprus has run some checks for me. A team with Vatican passports arrived two days ago. He did me a favour and called a friend in the local police. She told him they were staying as a group of tourists camping near the village."

"Which village?"

"The one still talking about the gun battle in the middle of the day. Some of the inhabitants still think the Greeks invaded again."

The Friar managed a small smile; it fell instantly. "OK. So they're getting close. Too close. The location of the capture was a secret known only by the order and the Office of the Holy See."

"I doubt the order would have told them, or they'd know where we buried him. A leak in the Holy office?"

"Maybe there wasn't a leak. The war needs both sides. They'll think of the monastery soon. We need to get to him quickly."

"And when we get there? What do we do then?"

"We move him."

"Just the three of us?"

"Yes. Just the three of us."

Chapter 31

A reason to save the world

Hemal left me alone again. I remained at the edge of the abyss, gazing into its depths. I amused myself by probing the membrane. The thought occurred to me: if I solved that particular riddle I could escape this monastic prison. I noticed a strange change as I forced my will against the slick veil. The forms pressed against the onyx skin now avoided my presence.

When I first explored the abyss, they would press against the barrier, as if eager to reach me. I sensed a hunger in them. Now they avoided me. I sensed they feared me. I couldn't figure why, the only change I was aware of was my new found calm. Why that would scare these lost souls, I had no idea.

Venet disturbed my contemplation. I wasn't surprised to see him. Hemal had failed to convince me, now he would try. I was curious to see what approach he would take.

"What happened to the café ?"

"Didn't Hemal tell you?"

"No, she's back at the front line. I just wanted to see how you are."

He'd never been nice to me before. I guess that showed how desperate they were.

"I'm good, a little thirsty."

That slight gesture and a glass of water appeared in my hand. As always the simple beverage tasted good. I really did wish I knew how they did that. My lack of understanding didn't spoil the taste though.

"So why dismantle the café ?"

"I don't need it anymore."

"Really?"

"No, it was an illusion. It gave me focus, helped pass the time.."

"What changed?"

"Me I guess. The emptiness no longer matters. Besides I have you two for entertainment."

He scowled at my jibe. "Maybe not for much longer."

"Of course, the Apocalypse. The end of the world."

"Hemal told you what will happen?"

"She did. And I can't wait." My smile deepened his frown.

"What do you mean?"

"Well it seems to me this is my way out of here."

I let my smile broaden.

"I don't understand?"

"It's simple." And I had given the matter some thought. "When the world is ripped out of the universe, we'll all be transformed into souls. Then I would be free of this prison."

"Free to do what exactly? And why are you so certain it will free you from these walls?"

OK, maybe I hadn't given it enough thought.

"Either way I'm no worse off."

"You might be. In the physical universe these walls would eventually crumble. In Heaven you'd be trapped forever. And with the miracle inside you, it really would mean forever."

That wasn't a pleasant prospect.

"I'm here forever anyway."

"Thousands of years are a very long way from forever. I have existed for longer than the life of the universe, so I know."

"And the alternative is?"

"You can stop the Apocalypse."

"Why would I do that?"

"To save the world, I don't think many people have done that twice."

"Really? You're trying that line on me? That tactic didn't work for the Friar and it won't work for you."

"It will get you out of this prison."

Now that did interest me.

"True freedom?"

"Of course."

"What exactly do I need to do?"

"You need to kill the Antichrist."

"Of course I do."

"I'm serious. And you have to kill him before he opens the seventh seal."

"What happens if he does?"

"Then Lucifer will reign on Earth and he and Michael will kill every living human being when they move the world into Heaven."

"OK. Who is he?"

"I don't know. You'll need to find out for yourself."

"What do I get out of it?"

"I've told you. You'll get your freedom, to see the world again."

"It's not enough."

"I don't think you appreciate what the coming Apocalypse really means."

"I think I do. The end of the world. Death for every human on the planet. Except me."

"And the enslavement or destruction of every soul that has ever existed."

"And that means what to me?"

"I don't care what you think it means to you." I felt his anger wrap around me. "You have a duty to perform and you will do it."

I've never been one to bow to pressure. Although the look on the angel's face did worry me.

"I see you will need convincing. Let me show you what is in store for you if you refuse your task."

Venet's rage swallowed me whole. Darkness consumed me with a chill that almost quenched the miracle's fire.

Then nothing happened.

I explored the pitch black. I soon realised my senses provided no input. Like a good monkey I heard nothing, saw nothing. I reached out into the darkness and touched nothing. I inhaled, but smelled nothing.

Time passed.

As when I was first imprisoned in the wall I counted time. I counted the seconds until frustration gripped me and I shouted for attention.

I didn't hear my own voice.

More time passed.

I attempted to create a new sanctuary for myself, but in this darkness my will failed to grip anything. I was truly alone in this emptiness.

Yet more time passed.

"Do you understand yet?"

The voice shattered the darkness and for an instant I thought it was the voice of God himself. Of course it was Venet's voice. I nodded my surrender.

"Ok, I'll do it. I get the point. I don't want to be trapped here for eternity."

He smiled.

"How do I get out of here?"

"Knock knock."

Chapter 32

Heal thyself

I felt myself being dragged back into my flesh. Familiar agonies seared through my body as the miracle accepted me back into its embrace. As I was wrenched from my oasis, I heard Venet whisper a name. I didn't quite catch it, the name eluded me and then the pain reigned supreme and my concentration fragmented. Not since consuming the miracle had I hurt this much.

My own screams, weak and feeble scratched at my ears. A booming noise followed the rhythm of Venet's flippant comment, pounded the stale air around me. Something was happening. I tried to focus on this new external presence which disturbed my solitude.

I cast out my mind to find out. The miracle's grip weakened my attempt. The cold metal mask defeated the will that remained.

More noises. Now I recognised the bass of a hammer against stone, each blow louder than the last. After each strike I heard the softer sound of the shards falling to the floor. One blow landed, then another after a few seconds. With each impact the miracle clutched me tighter.

What did it know that I did not?

Another thundered impact and after the noise I felt a faint breeze upon my neck. The soft caress sweeter to me than any lover's kiss had ever been. I now made out breathing which wasn't my own. I thought I heard voices, but they were muffled by the mask. More stones fell to the ground.

Without warning, strong hands gripped me. They supported me as the chains were removed from my limbs. Another pair of hands pulled at the mask. Fresh torment as the mask tore away some of the skin from my face. I screamed a pathetic noise. My voice sounded less than that of a mewing animal. This new physical pain was raw compared to the fire of the miracle's embrace.

With the mask removed, the voices became clearer. I thought I recognised the gruff tone. I attempted once again to cast my will, but I lacked the strength. The strong hands pulled me from the wall. I realised I no longer heard chanting. I smiled, only to trigger new pain as the skin around my mouth cracked open.

I realised it was stupid, but I tried to open my eyes anyway. More torn skin and a light so bright I screamed again. At least here I noticed some improvement. I heard the feeble cry. I also started to make sense of the words being spoken around me.

"Is he OK?"

A familiar voice. A memory from what seemed so long ago.

"We need to move him now."

Another voice I recognised.

I passed out, this time into actual sleep.

* * *

I came to lying on a comfortable bed. I luxuriated in that sensation for minutes before stirring. This time the light merely dazzled me when I opened my eyes. I blinked as they watered with the strain. Within a few blinks they adjusted. My first sight was of an old man, a priest by the smell of him, he sat in a chair beside me. When he saw me awaken he stood up and without a word left the room. I closed my eyes to rest them for a moment and then I took advantage of the time alone to scan the room.

The bed and the chair were the only furniture in the room. A curtain covered the window, dimming the light. In my current state I was glad for that. The lack of bars on the window pleased me. The smell of fresh bread wafted into the room. The smell transported me back to the farmhouse before the battle with Lazarus. Hunger pangs also bit deep with the tempting smell.

The Friar entered the room. He carried a tray laden with bread and a steaming bowl. I think I almost fainted with desire. I sat up, only to collapse back on the bed as a wave of dizziness swept through me. I experienced some confusion on seeing Friar Francis.

First and foremost I felt rage. Here stood the man who had locked me in the monastery wall. Imprisoned me to what felt like an eternity of suffering.

I know, I know. I brought the judgement on myself stealing the miracle in the first place. The Friar guessed my plan to steal it, so why didn't he warn me?

Would I have listened?

Yet he had also freed me. For his own purposes admittedly, but all the same I was glad to be free. I surged my will against his mind just for old time's sake. I lacked the strength to do any more than brush against his defences.

He smiled. "It's good to see you again."

I couldn't reply. My mouth was too dry.

"Just relax. You're still weak. Here, drink some of this."

I sipped the offered water. Only then did I notice the tubes inserted into my arms. The Friar caught my look.

"The miracle sustained you, but only enough to keep you alive. You've suffered extreme muscle and tissue damage. Ordinarily it would take months to heal properly. However if you're willing, we can speed things up."

I drank the water; the water tasted as good as the drinks created by my visiting angels. I'd already decided I wasn't going to try and be clever this time. I'd kill the Antichrist as I'd done with Lazarus. To do that I needed my strength, so I simply nodded.

He studied me for a moment and then nodded himself. He turned to the old priest who had followed him back into the room.

"This is Father Moran. He can teach you skills which should help your recovery."

I nodded again.

Father Moran sat in the chair by the bed. He took my hand. Despite the priest's age, he possessed a strong grip. His hand also felt warm. Warmer than I expected.

"I'll leave you to it," the Friar said as he left.

I cast my mind out again, searching this time. Almost instantly I sensed who I was looking for. Hammond was still with the happy band. The joy I felt surprised me somewhat. Maybe the time alone had made me soft.

I turned to face Father Moran and he looked back calmly. "Let's begin," he said. "Friar Francis has told me about the training he'd given you previously. While I'm not as gifted as he, I have picked up a trick or two over the years."

I brushed my will against him. His defence felt feeble, but behind the shield I sensed the rock. The same rock I first discovered in Hammond's mind back in my first prison. This rock was different. All the ones I had encountered before sat in the centre of the person's being. This one towered like a mountain, filling his mind. The faith of this priest was staggering.

He might not be as powerful as the Friar, but he still sensed my probe and smiled.

"If you want to look in my mind, then all you need do is ask."

I lay back on the bed.

"All right then let's begin. We have two possible ways of healing your body. The first is to delve deep and repair the damage directly. From what I've been told this shouldn't be a problem for you. However, I think for you the second approach will be better."

I finally managed to speak. "And that is?"

"We should take a more holistic approach. With your raw talent it would be the quicker way. Now lie back and picture your body, the image should be of you as a healthy person. And then pour your will into that form."

"Is that all?" I felt more than a little disappointed. I expected something more complicated. Something more profound.

The old priest chuckled.

Chapter 33

That familiar feeling

I should have listened to his laugh. The method sounded simple and at first I found it so. Well, for the first hour at any rate. I did as he instructed, I lay on the bed. He attached a fresh glucose drip to my arm and told me to relax. I floated above myself and looked upon my emancipated form.

I looked terrible. Gaunt and faded like a third world famine victim. It pained me to see myself in such a weakened state. I hoped this technique would work. I needed to become myself again. Following Father Moran's instructions I focused my will into the wasted body below me. I pictured my form, healed and fit as I remembered it.

At first the task was as simple as I'd assumed. My will sank into the hungry flesh. All too quickly my strength drained away. Within minutes I lacked the strength to continue and retreated back into my body.

"Harder than it sounds, wasn't it?"

I simply nodded; even that small movement caused a dizzy spell. He patted my shoulder and left the room.

And so began a new routine. I'd wake and Father Moran would be waiting for me, or would enter the room soon after. He provided food and refreshments. Gradually I ate more and my strength slowly recovered. Once I'd eaten he'd tell me to lie back and relax. Again and again I poured my will into my flesh, boosting the healing. Each time I managed to last a little bit longer.

We repeated this for a week until I had enough strength to leave the bed. The change was miraculous, only when I left the room did I understand Father Moran had been aiding my efforts all this time. He looked drawn, dark lines shadowed his eyes.

On my first journey beyond the bedroom I found the Friar and Hammond in a small study. On the desk I noticed an odd looking book.

"It's good to see you up and about," Hammond welcomed me.

"I feel better. What's that?" I pointed at the book.

"It's about you," the Friar replied. "The book tells us what you need to do."

"I need to do?"

"You don't need to be coy. You talk in your sleep."

That surprised me.

"It's a good job you do. You filled in the blanks with what we first thought to be ramblings."

I pulled over a chair and sat down. I did feel better, but my strength still hadn't fully returned.

"So what did I say?"

"At first we weren't sure. You were arguing with somebody. We don't know who."

"Then you started saying a name. You kept repeating it," Hammond said.

"Whose name?"

"That was the strangest part. You kept saying 'Pierre Roux'. Over and over again. We had to sedate you to make you stop."

I shook my head. "I don't know the name."

"That's the interesting part," the Friar resumed. "The book told us what you have to do."

"Kill the Antichrist?"

"Exactly. Unfortunately the text didn't reveal who."

"You think it's this Pierre guy?"

"The name surprised us. In fact we didn't believe it at first."

"What do you mean?"

"You really don't know the name?"

"I've been locked in a wall for God knows how long. Why don't we skip that, before I start remembering how I got in that monastery wall?"

"You brought that upon yourself."

"Yes I did. And the fire which scorches through my whole body is a constant reminder. I have my eyes on a bigger prize right now. Let's keep it that way."

He nodded.

"Pierre Roux is the President of the European Union."

"So he's a big fish."

"That he is. He's also the man who has been making sure the conflict in the Middle East has been growing steadily hotter for the past three months.

"None of us realised how integral he'd been in creating the conflict. He's charming and persuasive."

"That hardly seems like proof he's the Antichrist."

"True. But with your naming of him we dug into his background a little more."

"Wouldn't somebody have already done so before he became president."

"Yes, but we believe he had people in place long before he ran for office."

"People in place?"

"This is the Antichrist we are talking about. This is the fruition of a plan thousands of years in the making."

"So you're certain?"

"Yes. Investigating events around the world we now know he has opened the seals. It was so obvious with hindsight, but he did cover his tracks well."

I remembered the seals from reading the Bible back in prison. "OK. So how many seals has he broken?"

"Six. He only has one more to open."

"All right. So how do we get to him? If he's the European big cheese he's going to be well protected."

"That's what we've been looking into," Hammond said. "Unfortunately it's even worse than that. To break the seal he has to perform a ritual. We don't know the details, but we do know where and when."

"Sounds good. Where is it?"

"It's a manor house in the south of France."

"How do you know that is the place?"

"The location didn't come cheap. We traced his phone's GPS history."

"And?"

"The history showed he visited this location on key dates. Key dates significant for satanic cults."

"I guess that's how we know the when."

"Yes."

"So when is it?"

"Three days. And we have to kill him before he completes the ritual."

Chapter 34

To kill a son

Hammond's contact arranged a Royal Air Force transport to fly us from Cyprus to a French airbase near Marseille. It wasn't the first time I'd flown, but it was the first time I'd flown while conscious. I enjoyed the novelty of flying even though it wasn't the most comfortable flight. The three of us hardly filled the cavernous expanse of the plane. Simple seats bolted to the floor provided little comfort. For safety they faced backwards.

I was surprised at how loud the engines sounded inside the plane. With the noise and rattling of the airframe, I found it difficult to concentrate. We didn't have much time. The flight had taken a day to arrange. Securing Pierre Roux's itinerary proved tricky and ultimately unfruitful. We did spot a pattern of appointments that matched relevant dates, they didn't provide any clue as to the location.

The Friar spoke with his contacts without any success. The head of his order did reveal the effort to find him and the rest of us had intensified. The order's offices had even been searched by the internal investigations unit. The Jesuits had joined the outcry when their offices were also searched. Father Moran was now listed as a fugitive and accomplice to Friar Francis.

Father Moran experienced better success. The Jesuits had learned of a coven in the south of France. They'd also gained access to the GPS trace history for the President. They didn't explain how and no-one cared to ask. The records showed Pierre visited a country estate periodically. Checking the dates Father Moran confirmed almost all of them corresponded to significant dates in the satanic calendar.

So now we flew to a nearby air base. Hammond reviewed satellite images from a French spy satellite. The estate was situated deep in the countryside. He'd already commented they had no time to plan, this would be difficult.

For my part I still felt weak. I was up and about, able to walk under my own steam, but lacked the stamina I once possessed. My time alone caused other changes, unsettling ones. I knew what I had to do, but this would be different. Lazarus had been stronger than me, but then we had a plan. Now we were out of time and were charging in without any preparation.

Don't get me wrong, I'd never been one for planning in advance, but I wasn't stupid. The plan had evened the odds last time. This time we'd have to rely on surprise. We all hoped that would prove enough.

My other concern was this Pierre Roux, the Antichrist himself. I understood nothing about him, beyond what I'd read in the Bible and from Venet's whispered words. All they had achieved was to identify the enemy. Lazarus had built himself up as a power over centuries. But this man had been born for this task.

All too quickly the flight ended. The sky was still dark when we arrived at the air force base. A local Jesuit contact drove us to the perimeter of the estate. He also provided weapons which Hammond and the Friar took. Father Moran declined. He looked strange and ill at ease wearing the black combat suit. I suggested he shouldn't come, but he'd firmly insisted.

I took a pistol. I wasn't trained, but I'd rather I had a weapon to hand if it all went to shit.

The driver dropped us off by the wall which enclosed the estate. The wall was concealed by trees, but the inner limbs were kept trimmed to prevent their use in scaling the wall.

Hammond scouted the wall, searching for a way across or any sensors. He found no sensors so the driver backed the 4x4 up to the wall. We clambered onto the roof and over the wall. There was a long drop down the other side. Hammond and the Friar lowered the Father down and then me. I already felt out of breath just with the excitement.

The land beyond the wall lay flat, exposed to the silvery light of the moon hanging low in the sky. As I caught my breath I looked upon the sky, where once I saw only wonder now I sensed only menace. I'd come to know how fragile this awesome reality was.

We all felt too exposed. We saw no cover to conceal our approach to the huge manor house standing proud on the horizon. Hammond led the way cautiously. We didn't have much time left. We had barely a few hours at best. Both Father Moran and I soon slowed the pace, both of us struggling for breath. The Friar stayed with us while Hammond scouted ahead.

It took us over an hour to cross the open space. Each moment filled with the dread of discovery. We crept through the yellow pools of light scatted around the building from the lit windows. We circled the building, Hammond still leading the way.

At the rear of the structure he stopped. We joined him and looked upon the garden. The space formed a circular shape with trimmed bushes. Flickering torches lined the perimeter. Inside, on a short cut lawn, a rank of robed figures stood in a semi-circle before the altar. Dressed in black we heard the low drone of their chants.

The altar itself stood on a small mound, so it was raised above the assembled worshippers. Behind the altar we saw a man robed in red. His hands were raised towards the sky. He didn't chant but stood still watching his followers.

Hammond took aim.

"We'll take him down. You two get to him quickly.." The Friar whispered. "I'll come with you and provide cover. Hammond will do the same from here."

"What do we do when we get to him?"

"Check that he's dead. If not put a bullet in his brain." He looked at Father Moran. "If he's possessed then bullets won't be enough. We won't have long, there's bound to be guards here."

Why haven't we seen any? A sudden itch at the back of my head needed scratching.

Father Moran nodded and the Friar continued. "If he is possessed, we don't have much time. He..." He indicated towards me. "... can help you. He can fight the demon directly."

Hold on a minute.

"What do you mean directly?"

"You can battle him the same way you did with Lazarus."

That didn't sound good at all, but the choice had already been made. With a sigh I said, "OK."

"All right. Let's move!"

Hammond fired a single round. The bullet struck Pierre clean in the forehead. The President fell to the ground. The Friar charged into the group firing short, controlled bursts. Two of the chanting cultists fell to the ground. The others didn't react and continued their dark prayers.

Something felt very wrong here.

I followed the Father as he ran to the fallen Antichrist. Another single shot from Hammond dropped another cult member. We reached Pierre, I touched him and his eyes opened.

"It's good to see you. We've been waiting for you."

Pierre stood. I aimed the pistol and shot him. At that range I didn't need any training. He grimaced with the bullet's impact. I fired again. He grabbed the pistol before I could pull the trigger again. He smiled at me.

"Abomination!" Father Moran hissed. He reached into his jacket for the vial of Holy Water.

"We'll have none of that," Pierre grabbed the priest's face, pushed his hands into the old man's mouth and pulled. I heard the snap of the priest's jaw as he fell screaming.

I noticed the gunshots had stopped. I spun around. The cultists continued to chant, but the Friar had fallen to his knees clutching his head. Further away several uniformed guards beat Hammond to the ground with their batons.

I turned back to the Antichrist. He still smiled at me. He levelled the gun at the old priest. The gunshot deafened me so I didn't hear my shout. I hadn't known the priest for long, but he had helped me.

"We've been waiting for you. We've never met, but I've always known you'd be here for this moment. Nobody else would do for this final sacrifice."

I did the only thing left to me. I drove my will into his mind.

Chapter 35

The Devil's trap

His smile followed me all the way in.

He offered no resistance, put up no defences. I recalled the first time I'd entered Hammond's mind. His too had been completely open. The only impenetrable part had been the rock at the centre of his being. Here I found not a rock but a mountain.

His faith formed the black mountain that towered above me. The obsidian exuded cruel menace, a coldness which sliced through my will as if it were a wind of razors. I strengthened my resolve and pushed in further. The wind continued to tear at me. The shredding gale wasn't an impediment, only an expression of this creature's joy to see me.

At the foot of the jagged mountain I encountered a familiar fallen angel.

"Venet."

"I'm pleased to see you've arrived."

"Hemal too?"

"No. She was a necessary subterfuge. Helped me sell the story if you like."

"I thought you couldn't deceive each other?"

"You shouldn't believe everything you hear. And besides, you humans have taught us many wonderful things. Deceit being one of the most useful."

"Why all the deception?"

"We didn't know where you were imprisoned. We needed the good Friar to come to your rescue. Then lay a little groundwork so you'd come to us."

"So no freedom then?"

All right, I did feel a little disappointment.

"I'm afraid not. You will be in a lot of pain until the moment you die."

"And then?"

"Even more pain."

He didn't look too upset about the prospect.

"But the miracle – how can you kill me?"

"I can't. But he can," he indicated the mountain behind him.

"So what are you…?" And in that moment I realised. I rushed to return to my body.

"Too late," Venet told me. I seemed to be surrounded by smiles again. "You always were a little slow."

I responded by striking at him with my will.

He laughed.

I launched myself at him. He caught my charge easily and threw me to the ground. Pulling myself upright I lunged at him again. He let me wrestle with him for a while. Long enough for me to feel my strength fading and then cast me down again.

"I can and will do this all day. In fact, I've been looking forward to it."

He kicked me along the ground.

I speared my will at him, visualising the attack as a firestorm engulfed him completely. I poured more of my weakening will into the flames.

Above the roar of the fire I heard his laughter.

He stepped from the conflagration.

"I've suffered more intense fires than that. You know, I wasn't one of the original rebels. I fell quite a bit later. Do you want to know why?"

I stood again. He knocked me back down.

"No? Well I'll tell you anyway. It's because of you."

"Me?"

He kicked me again.

"Not you personally. Your kind. Primitive and dirty, you taint Heaven with your presence. Everything was OK when you were just a curiosity in a toy universe. But your imperfection was allowed to pollute our existence. At that moment I realised God had abandoned his creations and he'd created you to torment us."

His enraged speech gave me a moment to recover. I dodged his half-hearted attempt at kicking me again. I wasn't thinking straight. In my state I couldn't fight this angel. I needed to get back to my body.

I ran.

And was smashed back down as he teleported in front of me.

"No escape that way."

He kicked me again. He put some real effort into the kick this time. In the physical world the blow would have broken several ribs. It still felt like he had.

"Don't worry. It'll soon be over. Then you'll no longer be anything special. You'll be another soul of many to feed Lucifer's army."

"Feed?" I gasped.

"Yes. We're purifying Heaven of your filth. Your souls are good for only one purpose. Consumption."

"What about the souls who already serve?"

"Food. Heaven will be cleansed. Powered with billions of souls we'll overwhelm Michael's armies despite his numerical advantage. Michael and his armies will be destroyed and only we will remain."

I teleported, using his own trick against him. I actually managed to escape. Then a pain so savage I nearly lost all conscious thought dragged me back to my flesh.

I opened my eyes to see the face of the Antichrist staring down upon me.

"Did my servant keep you entertained?"

I tried to move, only to find myself pinned to the altar. The warm light of candles and torches illuminated the scene. I couldn't see the Friar or Hammond.

"I'm sorry. Did you want to say goodbye? Well it's too late."

That fucking smile again.

A tsunami of rage surged within me. I unleashed a torrent of will against the gloating face. He absorbed my fury with the same shit eating smile.

"You taste good. I'm really going to enjoy consuming your soul."

He placed his hands upon my bare chest. Only now did I notice the cool breeze. From his burning hands tendrils of will snaked into my flesh. A searing network of strands permeated my entire being.

With a single movement he tore the miracle from my being and in that instant I died.

Chapter 36

The seventh seal

Revelations chapter 16 verse 1
And I heard a great voice out of the temple saying to the seven angels, Go your ways, and pour out the vials of the wrath of God upon the earth.

Pierre Roux looked down upon the bloodied form of his enemy. It was difficult to imagine this was the man spoken of in the prophecy. He'd expected the Deathless Man would have presented more of a challenge. Had Lazarus really been killed by this frail looking man?

He remembered Venet telling him of this man and his ordeal trapped in the monastery wall. The thought pleased him that his enemies had helped him in his work. However, he did feel a little disappointment.

After tearing the miracle from its thief, he subjugated it into his own power. Only the gifts of his Father rivalled the strength of the miracle. The fire of its existence teased his flesh, as the miracle merged into his being. His own strength and that of his Father suppressed the miracle's resistance and now he felt only the security of its embrace.

No force on Earth could stop him now.

The Antichrist gazed down upon the ruins of his enemy. A still mess of blood and torn flesh. He wouldn't deny the power he had gained from this enemy. Without him the purpose of his life might have been thwarted. How different would fate have been if this weakened man had run?

He snorted. These were foolish musings.

Helen approached the altar.

Pierre turned to face the survivors of his sect. Their chants now shouted towards the night sky. He felt his might mingle with the energy released from the sacrifice. He too faced the sky. Around him the vortices of energy twisted and reached into the heavens. Of the assembled people, only he discerned the tendrils of power which cavorted with eager purpose.

This was the energy he required to bring his Father into this doomed world. Already he sensed the physical universe twisting and deforming around him. The great weight of Lucifer's being forcing itself along the hurricane of energy that filled the sky.

"You have done well my son."

The voice tolled like a bell inside his head. Only he heard the voice, yet the cultists all fell to their knees with cries of praise.

"Father. I live but to serve. Your time among us is here. We are ready."

"Yes you are my son."

Only then did Pierre Roux learn the terrible secret which had been kept from him all his life. A detonation of pain inside his skull drove him to the floor. Helen sat demurely beside him and provided small comfort. But in her eyes he saw the truth. She had known this was his destiny.

Helen had guided him throughout his life. She first told him of his importance, how he would bring the world into the bosom of his Father. She taught him what he needed to know to accomplish his task. From languages to accounting, then onto law and political history she steered him through the knowledge he now took for granted. It seemed to him, even now, there was nothing she didn't know.

Not only his mentor, she had been his guardian too. She baptised him with the blood of a childhood friend in the name of his Father. She introduced a world unseen and unknown by normal people. She helped him develop talents only dreamed of.

She'd taken his virginity on a cold October night and had been his lover ever since. She wasn't a jealous lover; she didn't mind his other partners. Sometimes she would join in, although that usually meant the end for the other woman.

And now she comforted him with a soft voice and cold eyes.

"Don't fight it. This is what you were born for."

He wanted to resist. Pride told him that he must. Her words soothed his mind. He screamed once as Lucifer's being shredded his mind and his duty was fulfilled.

Chapter 37

In the garden

Dying was a stranger experience than I expected.

One moment I was wrapped in the agony of the miracle being wrenched from my flesh. Then next I was transfixed in a state of metamorphosis.

They say when you die, your whole life flashes before your eyes.

That's true, but only describes a small part of it. The events unfolded from birth to the point of my demise. I watched my life with a clarity I'd never known while alive. I understood the significance of each choice I made. Second by second I comprehended the complex web of decisions and influences formulated around me.

With each passing moment I developed, not by the stream of my life's history, but by the thoughts, aspirations and fears I felt at the time. So this is how the soul develops, I realised.

Eventually the transition ended. I appreciated it wouldn't be the oblivion I sought, but it was still a bit unnerving to come to in the Garden. After the transformation I understood why people would be confused when they arrived.

The spot I'd arrived at was quiet, which brought some small relief. I also noticed I wasn't alone. The Friar and Hammond waited for me. A third figure waited with them. Despite her grievous injuries I recognised her.

"Hemal. What happened?"

"That bastard Venet is what happened."

"I know that feeling."

"He ambushed me when I came looking for you. I don't know how he managed to trick me, but I'll tear a piece from him."

"Will you be all right?"

"I'll heal in time. What does it matter anyway? I've failed to stop the Antichrist." I told them about Lucifer's real plan then asked. "Has Lucifer moved the world out of the universe?"

"Not yet, but we can't have much time."

"Much time for what?"

"For one last desperate attempt. Only God can stop Lucifer now."

"I didn't think he would intervene?"

"Somehow we need to make him."

"And how are we going to do that?"

"We need to find the only being not part of God's creation. We need to find the last true demon."

To be concluded in the final book of the trilogy 'The Last True Demon'...

Printed in Great Britain
by Amazon.co.uk, Ltd.,
Marston Gate.